THE TWO WORLDS OF DR. BEAUMONT

In his professional life he was like a machine—
precise, efficient and as steady as a rock. That's
why the other surgeons had it in for him. Given
to "sweats" and "shakes" during a difficult operation, they hated him for his calm self-assurance.
"He's hard and inhuman," they said. "A man
without a heart."

The three women in Surgeon Beaumont's private
life disagreed violently with his colleagues, for
they knew how tender, passionate and loving he
could be.

But suddenly both worlds were united in an effort
to stop Matt Beaumont from attempting what they
considered an "impossible" operation. Each
woman thought she had him hooked and wanted
to protect her future; each fellow surgeon knew
that if the "impossible" turned out to be possible,
he would be left in the shade.

AUTHOR'S PROFILE

A mid-Westerner by birth, Stuart Friedman has seen most of America
in his numerous travels and now lives in Indianapolis.

Among the various activities that have occupied his time are selling
advertising, working with a foundry maintenance gang, selling real
estate and the operation of a labor-industry counseling service.

He turned to writing as a career in 1938 and his first published book
was a well-received history of Indiana. He has written many stories
and articles for leading national magazines, and his books include
the current Monarch bestsellers NIKKI, THE FLY GIRLS and RASPUTIN:
THE MAD MONK.

A Compelling Novel

THE SURGEONS

Stuart Friedman

Author of RASPUTIN: THE MAD MONK

WILDSIDE PRESS

THE SURGEONS

Published in September, 1962

Copyright © 1962, by Stuart Friedman

Cover Painting by Harry Schaare

Chapter One

Dr. Matt Beaumont had begun the experiments after his surgical colleagues at Northside General Hospital voted "no confidence" on a risky operation he wanted to perform on his young patient, Judith Chalmers. Using twenty-six guinea pigs and thirty-four white mice, he'd chemically produced endocrine gland imbalances and the animals had developed disorders comparable to those suffered by his female patient.

Then, by stimulating or inhibiting pituitary, thyriod, parathyroid, adrenal glands and gonads in various combinations, Matt had brought the laboratory animals through several phases to their present robust health. Whether the experiments had begun in a spirit of defiance or science, they'd confirmed his diagnosis. The patient's cardiac, vascular, renal and hepatic problems that other doctors had been treating for years as primary were secondary, caused by her endocrine gland system.

The main work that last Sunday afternoon was microscopic analysis of blood, lymph and tissue specimens comparing earlier conditions with the current condition of his patient. When he took a break around three o'clock, his eyes were tired but he was in a state of exhilarating imbalance. And before the inevitable slow, gray tide of caution brought him back into balance, he wanted to communicate his surge of optimism. Unfortunately, Vicky, his fiancée and the quicksilvery delight of his life, was miles away.

Matt, a tall, solidly made, dark-haired man in his late thirties, stood up and walked back past tiers of caged rabbits, mice and guinea pigs toward the other end of the little basement lab in the hospital's old wing.

Even in this mood there was a look of gravity and strength about Matt's face, accented by the pattern of fine lines across his high, sloping forehead and a deep, slanting crease in the flesh between his eyebrows like a permanent frown line. His features had a spareness as though the skin had been stretched in straight planes down from the wide, prominent cheekbones to his jaw and blunt chin with a minimum of underlying tissue. While it was an exaggeration to say his face had taken on the blankness of a surgical mask, his expression was habitually controlled.

His face relaxed now as he approached the white-smocked figure of Miss Vassily, the young technician he'd borrowed from Pathology. Stationed with a stop watch at the treadmill where a white mouse was running with gusto, her head was tilted forward intently and she remained perfectly motionless when Matt reached her side.

It occurred to him that although for three months he'd spent parts of each evening and most weekend afternoons with Miss Vassily, he might not recognize her in a crowd. He was aware of her as a general type, a normally proportioned brunette of medium height and build, with a femininely rounded, youthfully attractive face like a million other healthy young women.

He knew fragments of her specifically, such as the quiet, slightly husky voice and the pleasing deftness of her fine hands in motion. But somehow he had no total individual image of Constanza Vassily. Despite unreserved recommendations by Walker and Jacobs who knew her work in Pathology, she'd originally impressed Matt as one of the dedicated types whose sense of a larger purpose inclined them to carelessness about small details. Since accuracy and precision were vital, he'd checked her closely in the beginning. He'd come to trust her absolutely in routine work. In the important matter of preparation of microscope slides, she was superb.

She took a reading from the recording device on the treadmill and wrote a number on a clip-board sheet covered with rows and columns of neatly inked figures.

"You'll find these interesting, Dr. Beaumont," she said, holding the clip-board up for him to see. "In nearly every case the final rate is almost double that in Phase Two." She smiled at him. "Just as you predicted."

"Even without the figures," he said, nodding at the mouse on the treadmill, "you can see she's in fine shape. The microscope confirms it, too."

"As soon as I've finished with the last three subjects, I could graph these figures. Charted, they'd be even more convincing."

While she was lifting the mouse out of the treadmill and

transferring it to a compartment in the portable cage Matt told her:

"You needn't bother with graphs. It would be well worth ignoring the opinion of anyone who has to have a picture drawn for him, considering the evidence we've got. Before you put XA-32 on the treadmill, Miss Vassily, I want to say I'm highly pleased with these studies and I know they wouldn't be the success they've been without the high quality of your work." He grinned at her. "Observe that I've said this and I'm still breathing freely. You can bear witness that I don't strangle on a compliment, especially a deserved compliment."

"Why, thank you, Dr. Beaumont," she said. She began to smile slowly, charmingly, pleased with him and with herself. "As to compliments, I thought you sometimes overpraised me about the microscope slides."

"Overpraised? And I thought I hadn't been giving you your due. Well, I've got an hour or so of work left. I'd better get to it." He didn't move. "You know when you smiled just then it set off a whole complex of thoughts: a healthy young woman's smile is a marvel of nature ranking with the endocrine system, and in fact, connected with that system; such a smile, reflecting an abundance, even extravagance, of vitality would be impossible to an organism in Phase Two of this experiment. In other words, your smile refocused into human terms the goal and meaning of the whole experiment, and it was suddenly easy for me to visualize my patient's face in the future, radiant and glowing."

"In the future, after the operation?"

He nodded.

"Dr. Beaumont, there's something on my mind. I know I must be foolish to imagine you hadn't thought of it, but . . . " She looked at him hesitantly.

"Go ahead, Miss Vassily."

"Naturally, you're not at liberty to disclose much to me and, officially, I know very little about the case. But you know how things get around in hospitals. I know there's strong opposition to your performing the operation, that other doctors want to manage the condition more safely, the way they see it. I don't have to tell you my position; I'm on your side all the way." She stopped and gazed at him, her dark eyes soft with concern. "But hasn't this experiment shown that the endocrine imbalance can be brought under control by chemical means, and mightn't that rule out surgery?"

"Yes. Surgery is contra-indicated—if these experiments are considered alone. But the patient has a kidney condition that would be seriously aggravated by one of the necessary drugs. Another of the indicated drugs—which was the wonder of the month two years ago—had been found to cause degenerative disease of the liver with prolonged use. I'm not about to let anybody start a new poison program for that girl," he said harshly.

"I didn't mean to make you angry."

"You didn't," he said tersely. He rested his palm on the curve of her shoulder and squeezed briefly. "It's not you, not at all."

He turned and walked away, his long stride quick with anger. He seated himself at the microscope and stared bleakly at the wall, his wide mouth drawn thinly. His neck was tense. He rolled his shoulders and massaged his neck. After a few moments he set to work.

The afternoon was gone and gray light showed in the frosted glass windows when he made the final notation on GP-26's history. At the same time Miss Vassily, who'd kept abreast with the filing, removed the last slide from the microscope and returned it to the slotted case. Matt saw she was out of her smock and in a trim powder-blue suit and her mouth was freshly lipsticked. He lit a cigarette and told her:

"I'll make out your voucher now."

She gave him a slip from her purse listing her overtime hours for the week, then went out in the hall. Evidently, from her frisky clicking sound, she'd put on high heels. Finishing the voucher for 22 hours, Matt opened his personal checkbook, deliberated a moment and finally decided on a $250 bonus for her. When she came back she had two paper cups of steaming coffee. She smiled and gave him one.

"Why, thank you. You must have read my mind," he said, taking the coffee.

"It seemed to me there ought to be some sort of ceremony," she explained.

"You're right!"

He touched his cup with hers. "Here's to the happy conclusion of a very satisfying job. It's been a pleasant relationship, Miss Vassily—personally, too."

They sipped their coffees.

"I must admit I was awed and scared of you at first. But it's been a wonderful experience. Satisfying someone with your standards makes me feel that I've arrived. I know the result will be another successful major operation for you Dr. Beaumont."

He gave her his voucher and the personal check. She was delighted, then uncertain.

"But isn't it really too much?" She frowned.

He shook his head. "I'm just sorry I won't be publishing so I could give you credit there."

"Well, thank you very much, Doctor." She paused. "I was wondering if it would be possible to let me know when the operation has been performed. Of course I'll be in touch with all your work, but I won't be sure which patient received the benefit of our work. I'll be relieved to know it's all over. From what I've heard it's terribly . . . well . . . uncertain."

He gestured impatiently. "I'll let you know. But the operation's not as dangerous as you've heard," he assured her. "What makes it controversial isn't a surgical problem at all."

"It isn't?"

"No, it's financial—the specter of a malpractice suit. I read a magazine item awhile back that sums up the situation. A doctor saw an accident on the highway involving a serious injury. He didn't stop. Had he administered emergency treatment and it failed to save the patient, he might have been sued for malpractice. In this city alone during the past year ten doctors have lost malpractice suits. Judgments against them ranged up to a quarter-million; several over one hundred thousand dollars."

"I remember. Some of the doctors were on the staff here."

"Yes. And I gave testimony in a number of these suits. Only three of the ten men were guilty of irresponsibility. The others were men of ability, integrity, experience. They exercised good judgment and managed the cases according to the best medical procedures. In some instances they had run out of proven remedies and were forced either to abandon the cases or resort to 'last hope' tactics. Financially, it

9

was their 'mistake' not to abandon the cases. But for the patient's sake they fought to the end. They lost.

"Their so-called fault was practicing their profession to the best of their ability. It ruined some of them. They're having trouble with malpractice insurance. Two of them lost their homes and everything they had. What it did to their emotions and their professional judgment is even more serious. And insidiously it's undermining all doctors.

"We're likely to think twice in the future before taking on difficult cases. And certainly we'll hesitate to try any new course of treatment, because a crucial point in malpractice suits is this: Was standard, approved, medical procedure followed? If a doctor can't back up his judgment by pointing to precedents for his efforts at therapy, he's defenseless.

"Fear threatens to paralyze us. Caution has to be a doctor's second nature, so far as that goes, but beyond a certain point caution becomes deadly. If I see a condition which, untreated, would be fatal and I refuse, for fear of failure, to undertake treatment, what am I? Not a doctor any more.

"If we're going to be intimidated to that extent, there's no hope for anything but regression to a new dark age in medicine. All research attempting to open up new areas would stop if no one dared apply the results. When new disease conditions arise requiring new techniques, they won't be developed if they can't be tried. You see?"

She frowned and said indignantly, "All advance, all progress would stop. It would be intolerable."

"The reason my own proposed operation has stirred up so much fear in this hospital is that it will be new. I've developed a technique for this specific condition. Since it's an original technique there's obviously no medical precedent for it. The hospital is afraid it might have a suit on its hands if I'm permitted to try it. I'm not afraid I *might* have a suit on my hands, I *will* have. Persons close to the patient promise me that if I go ahead with the operation and fail, they will sue for a nice round figure—one million." He laughed sourly. "Flattering. I doubt the judgment against me would run that high, but I don't doubt the judgment *would* go against me. I won't have a leg of medical precedent to stand on." He shrugged, finished his coffee and got to his feet.

She stared up at him with enormous eyes. She moistened her lips and shook her head, then hunched her shoulders. "I think it's dreadful," she said, her quiet, husky voice almost inaudibly low. "It's bad enough what a surgeon has to endure, performing delicate, highly skilled work under great tension and carrying with him every minute the terrible load of responsibility for life that goes with any operation. But then to have a sword hanging over your head in addition—it's unjust! It's outrageous! How you must have struggled to work out your new technique. As overworked as you are, with as little time and spare energy as you have, you put your heart, your brain, your knowledge, your best hopes into it. And now, after you've given yourself this way to save a life they would try to ruin you, as if the lost life and the failure of your best work wouldn't hurt enough."

Her intensity surprised him. He gazed into those deep, emotion-filled eyes. Involuntarily his hand came up and touched her face caressingly. The smooth paleness of her skin, the rich width of her full, high cheeks, the loveliness of her white forehead had a flower-like beauty and sweetness. He bent and kissed her forehead.

"Constanza, you're my friend."

Her eyes suddenly brimmed. She put her arms around him and held onto him, her head against his chest. "You're a good man, a fine man!" she said fervently.

He laughed softly, patting her upper back. He eased away, smiled down into her face.

"Ah, female emotionalism. It's why I wanted a male technician on this job . . . and why I'm damned glad I didn't get one."

Constanza laughed.

"I could kiss you!" As she said it she went up on tiptoe and her hands urged him to bend toward her. She pursed her lips and after a moment's hesitation Matt kissed her mouth. They separated after the briefest contact.

"The same as, but nicer than, a friendly handshake," she said.

"Agreed." He smiled at her.

The soft mood ended abruptly with the crash of a slammed door and the tiny whipcrack sounds of rushing spiked heels. A petite, vivid figure in a short, pink silk

11

dress charged in from the hall, shouting in a high, girlish voice:

"That's enough of that! Too much!"

It was Matt's fiancée, Vicky Lassiter.

"Let me do the talking," Matt told Constanza in an undertone.

Vicky came at them in a gorgeous fury, her shoulder-length, reddish-blond hair swirling, her skirt swishing with the agitated beat of her concealed thighs. She seemed to capture all the available light in the dim areaway. It gleamed from her red-gold hair, flashed from her emerald-green eyes, touched the long elegant lines of her lower legs and, gliding pinkly over her dress, defined the rhythmic, shifting contours of her graceful young body. Her small, round face, blending the delicate brow, the impudently uptilted nose and the nakedly voluptuous mouth, was challengingly pretty.

Normally the lower part of her face protruded slightly; her mood now accented the thrust, bringing her mouth forward like a tantalizing offer of ripe tropical fruit. Her primitive animal vitality radiated waves of excitement that sharpened him with pleasure, and his heartbeat quickened. She was a spice flower and a volcano, he thought adoringly —an elemental force.

When this mere 110-pound splendor of a girl had swung into his orbit seven months ago, she'd shifted the magnetic poles and changed the climate of his life like a new geological Age of the Thaw. He wondered anew what mystifying processes of hormones and fate had made her dismiss a loyal army of suitors and choose him. Far from deserving her, he hadn't had the wit or boldness to even approach her that night of the hospital fund-raising ball when he'd first seen her.

In fact, if she hadn't seen him and come to him and informed him that she wanted his head and would be pleased to have him deliver it to her apartment to be sketched, he would still be living in the Ice Age.

She reached him and stared up into his eyes, her hair settling like a frame of lights and soft shadow around her compelling face. A pulse fluttered in the kissable hollow of her throat and with each intake of breath there was a shimmer in the flesh above her conical breasts. He felt a beginning throb of the powerful sexual cravings Vicky always stirred in him.

"You were so wrapped up in each other you didn't even notice I was watching through the glass in the hall door —for three of four minutes! I couldn't believe my senses!" she said, her voice trembling with an effort to control her anger, her glance flicking repeatedly from him to Constanza. "You kissed her forehead. You held her in your arms. You kissed her on the *lips!*"

He tried to keep in mind her training as a singer, her experience as a little theater actress, her natural eloquence and tendency to heighten effects. But under the accusation in that last word was a note of anguish that touched him like a cry of the betrayed.

"I know, Vicky, I know. But it was just a little kiss." His voice and eyes caressed her. But he was alert, aware that she must be handled carefully. "You mustn't be upset, sweetheart."

"But I *am* upset. If I'd come here snooping, suspecting something, I wouldn't be so upset. But I had dinner all ready and waiting and I was so anxious to see you. I thought if it was taking extra time for you to finish up you'd be nervous from all the close work and not feel like driving. So I drove down thinking you'd be glad. Then I got to that door there and peeked in. I couldn't believe it. It was like the solid ground had started to shake and tilt under me."

She stepped back, her heels ticking daintily. She glanced down, up again. She studied his face and at the same time began turning his engagement ring around and around. For a panicky instant it was the ground under his own feet that seemed to slip. She let her hands drop, the ring safely in place. Whether or not she'd been bluffing he didn't know; he was never sure of her. Uncontrolled, her moods built to violent intensities and sometimes swung with frightening swiftness to opposite extremes.

"Vicky, you're building a trifle into . . . "

"I've got a say coming, Matt. Let me say it."

"All right, baby," he said. He reached out to touch her bare, pretty arm. She drew it back, shaking her head.

"I got teased about all the nights and weekends you've been spending on this extra work. Friends, relatives, would

13

laugh. 'Vicky,' they'd say, 'you're not so sharp trusting him. Don't you know how doctors are? You don't mean you're letting him spend all that time alone with that ballerina-faced, smoldering-eyed character; those quiet slow-fire, dark ones are the worst.' I'd laugh with them, and show this," she said, holding up her left hand, doubled into a small fist. Staring levelly at Constanza she wagged her fist, flashing Matt's three-carat diamond engagement ring. "I'd tell them, '*I'm* the one he put this on, and the only way another woman will get it is in the eye. In case she's got an eye left after I finish clawing.' "

She let her gaze drift back to Matt. "Just a little kiss, you say. Nothing to be upset about. But I want to know what's been going on between you two all these months. How, if it was all work, could a relationship develop to the point that you wanted to hold her and give her 'just a little kiss'?" she ended bitterly.

The assurance she wanted, Matt sensed, was not that he loved her, but that he respected her. He did, because when she wasn't in the grip of emotional excesses Vicky had character, strength and high abilities.

In a way her achievements were greater than his; he'd struggled to make it because he'd had to or perish. Vicky had had a choice. Born to doting, wealthy parents with social position and luxury at her fingertips, she had had to fight its temptations and take the hard way to make something of herself. Nonetheless she often felt she was insignificant to him compared with his work, and this thing with Constanza was connected with his work and must be played down and made casual.

"Nothing's been going on. I give you my word. We've scarcely been aware of each other as people."

"That's so, Miss Lassiter," Constanza said from a little distance back of Matt.

He glanced across his shoulder at her and shook his head faintly.

"Why are you muzzling her?" Vicky demanded.

He shrugged. "There's nothing for her to say. No reason to get involved in what, after all, is a personal matter between you and me."

"Oh, spare the lady, is that it? Well, I intend to hear from her."

"Come off of it, Vicky. That kiss hadn't the remotest connection with passion."

"No. It was tender. There was a bond expressed. A deep understanding. How to you explain it, Miss Vassily?"

"Is it all right, Dr. Beaumont?"

"Speak freely."

"Very well. I'm sorry, Miss Lassiter, that you had to see something that completely misrepresents the relationship we've maintained. It's been entirely on the professional plane."

"Until just now," Vicky said, her chin lifting haughtily.

"Yes. What I think happened was that now that the work's done on what's been a long job, we both felt celebrative. In that mood of relaxation we felt a certain natural sense of . . . oh, recognition, because of the shared experience."

"You hadn't even thought of him as a man?"

"I respect and admire Dr. Beaumont enormously. Nothing more. His attitude to me has certainly never gone beyond appreciation of my help. When, just now, he spoke of the serious difficulties that stood in the way of his work as a surgeon, my impulse to help him in the only way I could with understanding sympathy, was too strong to resist. I didn't think."

"You should have." Vicky cleared her throat, looked wonderingly at Matt. "It's worse than I thought. I've always known, no matter how convincingly you denied it, that women in the world of medicine had a strong attraction for you. They're associated with what you value highly and they take on some of its luster and meaning. Clever women know quite well how to cloak themselves in this larger thing outside themselves and exploit it."

"Oh, the way I moved in," Constanza said scornfully, "was more than clever. It was insidious."

"I know. Before the opening hug and sweet sexless kiss, you were just the dedicated little scientist living in an exalted atmosphere of truth and noble sentiment," Vicki said briefly. "Not neglecting, however, to splash your mouth like a raspberry sundae and to put some bedroomy shadow on the lids to give the dark eyes a little more zazz!"

"No, not neglecting to make up my face at the end of my working day. I also washed my hands, if that wasn't being too competitive."

15

Her challenging tone made Matt half turn toward her. She stood braced, her legs so widely apart that her powder-blue skirt stretched taut across the knees. She stared intently at Vicky.

"There's a note of hostility about you, Miss Vassily," Vicky said carefully, "and, I might add, an objectionable suggestion of proprietorship toward Dr. Beaumont."

"Pride, not proprietorship, Miss Lassiter, based on appreciation—*full* appreciation," Constanza said, her voice hoarse and fairly throbbing.

"You emphasize the word *full*. Meaning, perhaps, that I fail to give him full appreciation?"

"It's really no fault of yours," she said, condescendingly, "since you know Dr. Beaumont only outside the mainstream of his life."

"I *am* the mainstream of his life, you nasty cat," Vicky shouted. "I ought to slap your damned face off."

"Try it!"

Vicky fought for control of her emotions. Then said menacingly, "You stay away from him, Vassily. That's an order!"

"Both of you shut up, and *that's* an order," Matt said in a cold voice. "You step over here, Vicky. And, Miss Vassily, you can leave now." When she continued to watch Vicky he snapped, "Miss Vassily!"

She looked at him with the air of someone just coming awake. She nodded slowly, turned to get her purse, then walked past them.

"Good evening, Dr. Beaumont."

"Good evening, Miss Vassily," he said. He and Vicky watched her till she had gone out the hall door.

He looked at Vicky and started to smile.

"Baby, the way you played your scene from entrance to curtain—you're a credit to your little theater group."

She began to giggle, then wrapped her arms around his neck and gave him a hot, tongue-stabbing kiss.

When they separated Vicky said breathlessly: "Let's hurry so there'll be time between eating and your hospital rounds for some high voltage sinning."

Chapter Two

"I want to carry it," Vicky said, when Matt closed his brief case.

"It's got all these endocrine experiment records in it," he said, carrying it toward the laboratory door, "plus some case histories, a quarterly journal, a thick annual compendium on surgery, a——"

"Please," she said, hurrying beside him, "let me do it for you." She pried at his fingers.

He stopped and shook his head, looking at her with a softly indulgent expression. She was the picture of lovely frailty, the lines of her body somehow wilted. Her eyes delivered an eloquent, defenseless appeal.

"But, Vicky, it's too heavy for you."

"If it were a hundred pounds of jewels you had commanded me to carry as a gift to another woman, I would obey."

"You mean a hundred pounds of bombs," he bantered.

She didn't smile.

"I want to serve you. I must!"

"You win."

He was about to add some flippancy about her aggressive submission, but caught himself. Though he was usually an incompetent diagnostician where Vicky's volatile emotions were concerned, he was sure she felt important carrying his brief case. It symbolized his work and she was still touchy about Constanza's taunt that she wasn't in the mainstream of his life.

While they walked from the lab to the basement exit, she held the brief case in one arm and curled the other arm around his. The sensation of her small, warm velvety palm against his, the faint pressure of her fingers entwined with his and the enchanting virtuous expression on her face as she carried his burden was so potent he felt drunk with love.

"Know what I thought about you this afternoon?" he said when they left the building.

17

"Tell me."

"You're the quicksilvery delight of my life. D'you like that one?"

"Oh," she hugged his arm, "it just dances!"

The refreshment of the early spring air, the feel of her hand in his, the look of the hospital wings towering against the dusk ahead and to the right, gave him a vast sense of well-being as they crossed the nearly empty parking lot.

"You flavor, you sweeten, you bind everything together —the world, my work, my personal life. I feel whole, happy, more alive and stronger. Ah, Vicky, I'm so lucky to have you. You mean so much to me.

"Look," he said, his voice hushing. He stopped. "To me there's a special wonder, a beauty about the lighted windows of a hospital at just this time of the evening when the last of daylight's leaving the sky."

He looked down at her and she began to nod slowly.

"I knew you'd feel it, Vicky."

"Before I knew you I wouldn't have appreciated it or understood. I'm so proud of you and your work. I brag to everybody." Her smile faded slowly. "But sometimes I feel so unimportant, so unworthy. That's why I lost control when she said I was outside the mainstream of your life."

"She had no right to talk to you that way."

When they reached her low-slung white sports car parked beside his sedan, she said:

"Stay with me; don't take your car. I'll bring you back."

"All right, but I'll drive."

"Oh, no. Didn't I install the seat belts? Didn't I have the governor put on so I couldn't burn up the highways? And in the city I haven't been over forty in weeks. If *you* won't have confidence in me, who will? Please, darling, let me drive."

"O.K.," he said, laughing. He got into the right-side seat. "But you watch your speed, with me or alone, because I've seen the results of too many crack-ups not to worry when I think of you helling around the way you used to."

When she had settled herself in the seat, he reached over and belted her in tightly. She took the opportunity to nuzzle her cheek against his face and bite his neck lightly. Drawing away he saw her smirk.

"Feeling smug about getting your way?" he asked.

"About having you belt me in that protective way as if

18

I'm something precious." She laughed, then started the car and headed for the street.

"I could tell you things about how precious you are."

"Well, if I have to listen," she teased.

"This afternoon I was taking a short break and I had this enormously good feeling about the work. But I was frustrated. Why? Because I couldn't lavish that rich feeling on you. Everything connects with you, these days, or it isn't complete, Vicky. It's not only that I can't think of the present or future without you. I'd like to be able, somehow, to give you all the rewards I've ever had in the past: the sense of achievement and meaning and the good, clean strength every time I managed to overcome another obstacle when I was struggling to get my education and training . . . the deep satisfactions in the progress-without-complication of my postoperative patients . . . the expressions in the eyes of certain patients when they had begun to recuperate and emerge from fear and pain into renewed hope and life. Treasures like that are almost impossible to give, but I'd give them to you."

"And you never wanted to share any of those finest things in your life with any of your other girls, did you, Matt? Because it's really true, isn't it, that you never were in love with anybody till me."

"True."

To be his first real love was wondrous to her and she brought it up often. When they'd become engaged last Thanksgiving, Vicky had admitted to being in love a number of times.

On his part Matt explained that he'd felt grimly overdisciplined and afraid that his lack of a continuing, satisfying personal life might distort his judgment, harm his work; therefore he'd needed and wanted a wife, a home. So he'd tried unsuccessfully but repeatedly to fall in love, for years. Vicky hadn't appreciated his frankness, nor he hers.

The subject nagged her and through the months she'd constantly re-opened the question and re-interpreted his feelings. She'd first reduced the possible importance of previous women to that of a sort of extra scalpel in his surgical arsenal.

Then she'd convinced herself that he had never actually needed that extra piece of equipment; at no time had he *really* wanted to love or marry, not till he found her. She

19

took second looks at her own past and realized that, female-like, she looked on love as a cure-all and had tried to imagine herself in love. She'd chosen puppet men, invested them with a brief meaning and reality in order to solve a temporary emotional problem. She was now convinced that she, like Matt, had never before known real love.

En route to her apartment she poured out her day to him in a laughter-splashed, lilting flow of words, her lips shaping endless varieties of delicious red circles, ovals, mounds. She'd visited cousins and friends, gone to the three-acre building site of their new home in the Waverly Hills section.

". . . and except for the usual sour-grapers, everybody enthused all over the place about everything—the view, the grounds, the landscaping plan, and, of course, the plan of the house itself. They said they knew I'd love it when it was done and I said I did now and you did, too. I warned them it wasn't going to be a recreation center, because my future husband had special needs and my first consideration would be his interests and tastes and that our social life would be built to your specifications. Then we went to the club for a drink and a swim and I dashed home to get the meal ready and waiting. The rest you know."

"Did you get everything settled with Mason?" he said, referring to the architect.

"Oh, he didn't show up for the appointment."

"He didn't? He said he'd make it by two-thirty so you could show him that place in the foundation and those frames and louvers in the daylight; then he'd know what to tell the contractor before the crews got started tomorrow. Why, he gave me his word on the phone this morning that he'd be there. He's a dependable guy; I can't imagine what happened."

"Oh, two-thirty. I thought it was three-thirty," she said with exasperating casualness, and quickly changed the subject. "That reminds me, before I forget, Matt. You know who snubbed me at the club? It just makes me sick. Mr. and Mrs. Chalmers."

"The Chalmers? I'm sorry as the devil, Vicky," he said, the frown-line between his eyebrows deepening. Their daughter, Judith Chalmers, was the patient with the serious endocrine problem that he hoped to correct by surgery. They had blocked him from the first. Since Judith had become twenty-one and she could grant him permission to perform the operation she herself wanted, her parents hated Matt. They were the ones who'd threatened to bring a malpractice suit for a million dollars in the event of failure, hoping the threat would be enough to stop him. "How did it happen? What did they say?"

"Nothing. They just looked coldly through me. They were lunching on the terrace. I've known them since I was a little girl. So when I smiled and spoke, like always, and they looked at me that way I don't know if I was more shocked or hurt.

"I just turned red and walked off and wanted to cry. It was like an uncle and aunt had suddenly disowned me. In a way, they were like an uncle and aunt because I knew their Judy as well as a cousin. She was three years younger and sickly and not in my crowd, but I was never unfriendly to the poor little thing. If she wasn't around I'd inquire how she was, and there was, you know, a nice relationship.

"I admired the Chalmers. They have been people of position for generations. Then for them to do such a thing to me! It was petty, unjust. I'd hoped to be able to intercede in your behalf and get them to give up that idea of suing you. To be cut off from doing that hurts me worse than their hostility to me personally. Still, it may not be too late. I could make them listen to me."

"I don't want you going to them in my behalf. Don't let people like that hurt you, Vicky," he said in a low steady voice.

"People like *that*? Why, they're fine people. And they're terribly important."

"I know. They told me."

"You're growling!"

"Fine people!"

"Oh!" she wailed. She struck the steering wheel with her fist. "I've got you in a temper instead of making you happy. What am I good for?" She kicked her legs, her shoes clattered off. She bore down on the accelerator with her stockinged foot, zooming their speed from thirty to forty-five, roaring the low, powerful car in a snake line past traffic in center and outer lanes.

"Cut it out!"

"I wish I was dead!"

21

A block away the traffic signal gave a yellow warning; Vicky increased speed. The light flashed red before they reached the intersection and cars began to move across their path. Matt reached over and switched off the ignition, caught her right leg under the knee and pulled it back.

"Hit that brake!" he commanded, grabbing the steering wheel. "NOW!"

The sudden braking pitched them forward in the seat belts. The tires screeched; the whole vehicle wagged like a great tail. He jockeyed the car into the curb and stopped inches from the intersection. He opened her seat belt and his own, got out of the car, gestured abruptly for her to get into the right seat. He went around and got under the wheel, ignoring the gaping line of drivers at the stop signal.

"Buckle in," he told her, and watched to see that she did.

He neither spoke nor looked at her again till they were stopped in the parking area behind Bayle Towers, where she had an apartment.

She sat looking down in her lap. He found her shoes and put them on her. When she didn't lift her hands he unbuckled her. He got out, walked around to her side, and crouching, peered into her face. She turned away. He took her chin, turned her face to him.

"Don't look at me," she whispered. "I'm so ashamed."

Very softly, very slowly, he pressed his lips to hers. When he drew away and smiled at her, she looked at him mournfully.

"How can you love me?"

"It's easy. Come on. Let's go up and have a nice meal and forget it. You're all right, now. That's all that counts."

She sighed and let him help her out of the car. She leaned against him in the elevator with her eyes closed. Inside the foyer of her smart sixth-floor apartment she held onto him again.

"I've totally disqualified myself to be your wife," Tears oozed from her closed eyes. "I'm supposed to soothe and and calm and steady you for your work, not add to your tensions. Oh, Matt, I fail in everything."

"Now, sweetheart, not in everything. You haven't tried everything."

Her eyes flew open. She stared indignantly at him, then abruptly collapsed, laughing.

"Oh, that's wonderful. I was headed down into an orgy

of self-pity." She caught his wrists, drew his hands glidingly around and down her body. His hands curved to fit the rounds of her pert, ungirdled bottom. She grinned up into his face and whispered: "When I was gunning toward that intersection at fifty did it give you a sex bang, too?"

He shook his head slowly, solemnly.

"Not the teensiest?" Her buttocks clenched and she stepped out of her shoes and onto his. Her warm body began a circular motion against his and she opened her rich red lips slightly and shut her eyes. His mouth dropped like a hawk, covering hers. Her lips closed and opened, closed and opened succulently, and the yielding softness of her moving belly against his roused maleness dizzied him. They separated and stared into each other's glazed eyes. She mashed her body harder against his and forced open her lips. He kissed her hungrily. When they parted again his whole body was throbbing.

"Now," she commanded. "Spank me for being so naughty."

He struck a hard, sharp-cracking slap to her bottom.

"Again and again and harder!" She began to move her legs up and down in an excited dance. "Hurt me. Punish me. Love me."

He spanned her waist, lifted her bodily and set her away from his, shaking his head.

"I'll love you later!"

Her glance dipped down his body, bounced to his face. She grinnned.

"How can you wait?"

"Damned if I know."

"I know you planned on dinner first," she said. She plucked at her skirt and lifted it, tantalizingly a few inches above her knees. "So I wouldn't want to disrupt the schedule."

The skirt was rising up her thighs, inch by inch, nearing the edge of her panties. She watched him steadily, grinning. "I notice you have your fervor totally under control," she said sarcastically, and giggled.

"Think I can't resist you?"

"Uh-huh." She tiptoed backward. He moved forward.

"I'm fighting," he laughed, "but I'm losing!"

He reached for her. She danced back, laughing gleefully and dropping her skirt. He caught her by the arms.

"Truce," she said. "End of the round. Yes? No? Now? Later? *Oooooh*, you're wickedly handsome!" She caught her breath. "I can't wait. Make me wait."

"Suits me." He released her and reached for his cigarettes.

Vicky watched, entranced, as he lighted.

"It's fabulous. No matter how excited you are your hands never tremble."

"They can't. I disconnected them from my emotions long ago." She made him self-conscious about his hands, but he couldn't escape them. Vicky's sketches of them, with others of his face, dotted the walls of the front room and foyer.

Wide and proportionately thick, with broad, strong fingers, they were good hands but not extraordinary in appearance. There was little external evidence of the specialized development of nerve and muscle that gave his fingers the hyper-sensitivity vital to him as a surgeon. His delicately exploring fingers perceived more than his eyes, even when the operational field was open to his vision; he trusted his acute tactile sense more than his sight. In many cases he could have actually performed whole operations precisely and speedily with his eyes closed.

"If I were a man and had hands like yours I'd walk with them up in the air for everybody to admire."

"They're work hands," Matt said. "How about putting yours to work while I tell the hospital this phone number, check my answering service and get washed up? There really is a meal, isn't there? Or should I call the caterers?"

"I'll 'caterers' you," she said, stepping into her shoes. She swung around and walked toward the kitchen. "Is there a meal! Oh, and darling, maybe you shouldn't put off calling the architect and explaining what he has to tell the contractor . . ."

She vanished into the kitchen. Matt hesitated, then followed and pushed open the swinging door.

"You've got a habit I don't always appreciate, Vicky—having the last word as you go through a door. That last line of yours makes it sound as if I'm likely to be negligent in a matter that concerns our home, when, in fact, it was your failure to keep that appointment that makes it necessary for me to call tonight. Unless," he added ironically, "I can manage it during one of the six operations I've got scheduled in the morning."

24

She was standing by the oven, putting on an apron. When she had the bow tied she said: "My grandmother used to say a hungry man's a fussy man."

"Your grandmother in a play called *Farm Frolics*, as I remember." He looked at her with a mocking grin.

He went back to the foyer and used the phone. Staring at him from a frame on the wall was the first charcoal sketch of his face Vicky had ever made; in her opinion, not his, she'd never bettered it. It showed him full face and stern as Jove, the long flat planes of his cheeks, the bluntness of his chin, the frown around his eyes and the height of his forehead all subtly exaggerated. It was stronger and harsher than he felt he was and a damned sight nobler than he knew he was. Finishing the talk with the architect in a good humor Matt went back to the kitchen and looked in.

"Mason's taking care of it. It's O.K."

He kept a few clothes here and changed into slacks, sport shirt and moccasins. He washed in the bathroom, then prowled the big, bright front room that combined sofa, chairs and a curved sectional piece, with her draftsman's table, lamp and stool and an orderly chaos of stacked newspaper ads and recent proofs.

Off and on she did fashion ads for one of the department stores. Her current work was a group of women in sportswear with a couple of diminished male background figures, both of whom resembled him. He stood chortling.

Vicky, coming into the dining area with a casserole called, "What's funny?"

"Me in these ads."

"As you very well know from snooping through three years of my drawings, you always were there, even before I ever saw you. I went with various types of men, but they never showed up in my work. It has nothing to do with your being my lover. You're my ideal. Come on and eat."

The soup, shrimp cocktail, au gratin potatoes, roast beef, tomatoes, hot rolls and coffee were delicious, but when she marched in with a lemon whipped-cream pie he groaned: "Vicky, I can't."

"You just dare not taste this pie!"

"You made it yourself?"

"I sure did; I can bake seventy different kinds of pies, fifty-five cakes, twenty-five kinds of candy . . . I used to

25

sell things like that to raise extra cash when I wasn't more than ten or eleven. My mother thought it was common to know how to cook, so I had our cook teach me. And I can garden and clean house and iron frills.

"I wasn't going to be like all the rich kids I knew, getting their confidence from money and other people and not having anything of their own to back them up. I was on a pay roll as a bookkeeper when I was sixteen, for a while, to show I could do it, which was enough. I can get jobs in eight different fields, not including my professional theater. Maybe I could there, too."

"M'm!" he exclaimed after the first bit of pie. "You're absolutely what you claim, good at everything . . . but I'll save this for a midnight snack."

"There's plenty of everything for later when you're back from the hospital. Why don't you stretch out now? Then we'll just relax and talk for a while . . ."

"Let nature take its course?"

She bustled over and switched on one small lamp and turned off the overhead lights. He stretched out on the couch and almost automatically "took five." When he opened his eyes she was standing over him in a gold floor-length robe buttoned at the throat and nowhere else.

"Guess what I've got on underneath."

He slipped his hand under the robe at her knee, explored upward along her naked silky thigh. He came up into a sitting position. He pulled her forward and kissed her breasts while she gazed down at him, her lustrous hair falling intimately about her cheeks, and caressed his neck slowly.

"It's more comfortable in the bedroom, lover."

In minutes he was stripped to shorts and stretched on his back on her bed. The room was dark except for a glow from the front room. She lay on her side against him, her knee sliding out across his body.

"Ah, this is nice," Vicky sighed contentedly. "Love me slowly."

Turning, he kissed her mouth and let his hands wander over her delicious, bare body for a while, then he just held her and stared at the dim ceiling. He was roused, and the constant friction of her leg on him was powerfully sensual. He knew he wouldn't be able to hold back from full possession of her much longer.

26

"If," she said in a sleepy voice, "they understood that by hurting you they would be hurting me too, they wouldn't want to sue you."

"What?" he said.

"The Chalmers."

"I don't want to talk about the Chalmers, darling."

"I don't either. I want them off my mind. I didn't dare say it when you were reproaching me about not caring for our new home, Matt, but it was because of them that I forgot the appointment. Something in me must have said: 'Don't get too attached to it; don't let yourself love it this much because you'll lose it. The Chalmers can take it away from you.' "

"Nonsense!" He rolled toward her, buried his face against her neck, kissing it. He withdrew, kissed her cheeks, her silly nose, her lovely mouth. "No one can take anything away from my baby!"

"You wouldn't let them, Matt?"

"Of course not, darling."

"When I think of poor Dr. Anderson who lost his home —and the judgment against him was only two hundred and thirty thousand dollars . . . his poor wife almost had a breakdown. She's with her parents; she and the children."

"Really? It's that bad? Well, there's a fund. We can give him some more help. I'll see about it tomorrow. Don't worry, he'll get back on his feet. He's a good doctor."

"His wife's older, more stable than I am. I just pray I'll find the strength . . ."

"Now, Vicky, you're letting yourself imagine things. In the first place I'm not going to fail in that operation."

"You won't. I know you won't. But you've told me stories yourself about unpreventable things that can go wrong in the operating room. Oh, I just wish you weren't doing that operation."

"I have to, Vicky."

"*Have* to?"

"Yes. I promised Judith Chalmers. I told her I could do it. I believe I can do it. I must do it."

"But how can you know you can do a thing that no other surgeon in the world, not even the greatest—I don't mean, Matt, that you're not great, but . . ."

"This isn't the time or place to discuss it, Vicky, for God's sake."

27

"It may not be, but it may be. The thing that seems to make you so compulsive about doing that operation is that Judy's in love and engaged. In her present shape she couldn't really become a wife or mother. You want to give her a love life."

"A *full* life, Vicky. That's just what those fine people of yours, the Chalmers, can't bear to see her have. They love her so much that they'd rather see her miserable and half-alive and yearning herself into a state of desperation rather than give her up. As an invalid she'll always belong to them —just like their banks, mines, oil fields, railroads and insurance companies. These fine, important people!"

He sat up, then stood up, found his cigarettes and lighted one, his hand rock-steady, his sexual desire vanished. He paced to the bedroom door, back to the bed. She lay looking at him, her face puckered up.

"You hate me," she whimpered.

"Vicky, don't be silly. Can't you see this tears my guts out, this whole issue? To have you doubting me, siding with those people—" He broke off, walked away. She got hurriedly out of the bed. She came to him.

"Forgive me. Don't be angry. I'm sorry. You hate them, then I hate them. Come back. Relax. Lie down."

"I'll finish the smoke first."

"I'd do anything for you, Matt. But you don't have to do anything for me that you don't want to."

He went to the bed and lying on his side, enfolded her in his arms. She lay on her side, facing him, her leg lying on his, her perfumed softness as sweet as bliss to his senses. They kissed and caressed each other till he was roused wildly again. He turned her onto her back and prepared to possess her.

Suddenly she rolled from under him, drew her legs together and pulled her knees to her chest.

"What are you doing? Come back here!"

"Matt, no! With all that seriousness I just can't think about sex. I'm all out of the mood."

"I remember one time," he said, hoarsely, "when you were all out of the mood and I had to take you by force and you suddenly turned to fire. That's what's going to happen right now."

He grabbed her arms, pulled them free of her legs. He pried her knees apart, and rolled her onto her back.

28

"No!" she said sharply. "Let me alone. I don't want you."

He drew back. "Because I won't call off that operation?" he said slashingly.

"Yes!" She hoisted her upper body on her forearms and thrust her little face at him. "If you're more concerned about that girl than about me, yes!"

He sat back on his heels and stared at her.

"That's not the issue," he said, half-aloud. "It's a matter of professional obligation. You're being hysterical."

She sat up, then crawled to him. She stood on her knees beside him and put her arms around his head.

"I want to love you, Matt. I want you to love me. But I must know, dearest, that it isn't just sexual passion you feel for me, but all-out, deeply abiding love, that you possess me forever in your heart, cherish me above all women! I must know that you won't jeopardize my whole future—and yours—for the sake of—"

"For the sake of my professional honor?"

"If you're going to put it on that basis—"

"If you're going to put it on a basis of my submitting to you on this issue before you'll submit sexually," he said, "you, Vicky, can go to hell. Straight to hell!" He pushed her away and got off the bed.

In three minutes he was dressed. In four, he was moving toward the door, out of the apartment. He picked up his brief case in the foyer and stood listening, waiting for the sound of her voice calling him back. He felt his neck tense. Something just under his heart began to turn cold. There was a brief twinge in his guts and, just before he found himself crawling back to her, he pulled in a deep breath, opened the door and left.

Outside the building he started walking rapidly, his eyes staring. He felt hollow. He was chilly. He was sick at his stomach.

He couldn't draw his breath freely. He had to force it in his lungs. He came to a dead stop, seized with profound dread.

Oh, my God, he thought passionately, *if I've lost her!*

He couldn't stand that.

He could! But he'd rather be dead.

Like hell he would.

Don't move or you'll step on your face it's so long, he

thought, remembering a taunt of his gay 18-year-old Aunt Sally-Dee when he was three. He forced himself into motion toward a phone booth at the next street where he could call a cab to take him to the hospital.

"Cheer up, the worst is yet to come," she had usually added with casual heartlessness. If she paused to look at him he would fight to produce a grin and sometimes his efforts released a flood of her love and she'd swing him up, hugging and kissing him; at other times she'd reach down and sweeten his whole being by mussing his hair or patting his face. Oftener she said it on the move and the feel of her going away from him made him scowl at her back and blink back tears.

Afterwards, afraid that his Aunt Sally-Dee might never come back, that he'd lose her forever, that the worst *would* come if he didn't obey her and cheer up, but helpless to feel good inside, he would make his face cheerful anyhow. It was one of the earliest masks Matt Beaumont had learned to wear.

Chapter Three

He'd always mispronounced his Aunt Sally-Dee's name "salady" connecting her with delicious fresh fruit salads and spring salads, even after he knew they hadn't actually been named after her. She'd been his mother's sister with the same "sweetheart-shaped" face, brown velvet eyes, light-brown hair, delicate, almost translucently white skin and pretty figure. They had resembled each other so closely that Sally-Dee was sometimes called Anne-Marie's twin, even though there was five years difference in their ages.

But the times when his mother actually looked as young as Sally-Dee were preciously rare. Those times were usually during an "off" period in her marriage, when his father, after one of those bellowing, slugging, furniture-smashing rages, had walked out on them. His mother would return with Matt to her parents' home, promising him and herself that this time it was for good.

After a few days her real face would emerge from its swollen gloom, sparklingly lovely, her eyes alive, her voice song-sweet, her touch light and loving. Then the terror would leave his own body like an actual unfreezing, his heaviness and sense of clumsiness vanishing. He no longer played listlessly indoors, never letting his mother out of sight, but ran outside freely for vigorous play. He didn't need to recheck every few minutes, squinting and blinking nervously, to see if he was being watched from a window or doorway.

His mother and aunt chattered and laughed together a lot and he had the confident impression that they were continually praising and admiring him. Sometimes his aunt and his mother would have a giggle-fest. It might start at the supper table in the presence of his grandparents or while they washed dishes or fixed each others' hair. They'd fall into each others' arms laughing helplessly. They'd try to stop but by that time Matt would be laughing hilariously with them, joining in the fun, and his antics would set them off again.

31

The first of these joyous frenzies that he remembered had been when he wasn't yet three. He hadn't been prepared for the point when, inevitably, real tears began to mingle with their laughter and they collapsed in sudden tragedy. Their crying shocked him. He stared at them, paralyzed, and suddenly had to clutch his pants and pinch himself to keep from wetting.

That night he was afraid of the dark and he had one of the worst of his many, terrifying nightmares. He woke pitching wildly in a tangle of bedclothes on the floor, his whole body sweat-drenched, his face flushed, his teeth chattering. The lights were on. His grandparents and aunt were standing there, wakened by his screams. His mother was kneeling beside him, crooning, holding him while he shook as if chilled to the bone.

And soon enough the nightmare was real again, because the marriage was "on" again. They were living in an apartment and he was eternally either there or due to be there. When he sat at table with them, Matt shrank, watching, waiting, smiling warily when smiled at, speaking when spoken to. He ate, but even the food in his stomach seemed to poise, undigested and ready to bolt. His mother didn't lose her sparkle at once, but as day after day went by without violence he sensed her nervous anticipation. He almost began to want the worst to come and be done with. Almost, because when it did come it was always the end of the world for him. Through his sleep would come a warning sharpness of a voice at the edge of violence, or sometimes the violence itself—the thudding, sickening impact of her body hitting a wall or the floor. He'd wake, trembling, hearing her cry of pain and fright, then came the slaps and the ugly sounds of fist bones bruising her flesh and his brutal, cursing voice.

The sound of her pain, her terrible sobs, cut into him like fire and he held his breath, not daring to protest and worsen things. And then in spite of himself he would begin to stomp and scream. The two of them would rush into his room in their night clothes, she trying to head his father off, pulling at him, her face streaked and puffed and blotched, her eyes frantic. His father would bellow for him to get the hell back to sleep and bang the door shut. Later, dishes would smash, a chair would crash, mirrors splinter. More than once the police came.

32

For days after such fights, there would be that uncon-concealable mournfulness about his mother, a sickness and despair that weighed him with sadness and helplessness. His father would be more dispirited than sorry. But she could never leave him till her hopes exhausted themselves, because—Matt came to hate the word—she "loved" him and in his heart he "loved" her and could not help the things he did.

She assured Matt that his father loved him, too. When he would not believe this, she scolded him, and he would sink into a deep depression. Finally, Matt came to feel that if she didn't quite dislike him, she nonetheless found his heavy moods unpleasant.

Before he was five he'd shown himself to be not only an unpleasant little boy, but a coward too, without the spirit to raise his hands when his cousins pushed him around. All he did about it was cry. Then he learned not to cry, but he still did not defend himself; he was unlovable, ugly, not worth defending.

When he was six his mother left him for a while in the care of his grandparents. Aunty Sally-Dee was about to get married. She told him she'd decided to start her marriage off right by taking him along as her son. He laughed and hopped and danced. He hugged her. He kissed her. But she began to look so unhappy that he realized she hadn't been serious about taking him with her. He suddenly jeered: "April Fool's past. You're the biggest fool at last. I knew you were kidding me. You didn't fool me for one minute. But I sure did you! Oh boy, Aunt Salady," he shortled, "I put one over on you that time!" He ran to his room, but he didn't cry.

His mother finally did get a divorce when he was seven. They had lived alone together for a while, then with one and another of her brothers; since Sally-Dee's marriage her parents had taken a small apartment so there was no room for them there.

When he was nine and in the fourth grade, sitting in an arithmetic class at 11:04 one Tuesday morning in early March, a monitor came into the room. Matt went with her to the principal's office. There was his grandfather, looking very old; his skin as well as his hair was gray. He reached out and clutched Matt's hand and tried to speak and could not. He led Matt out to the car before saying a word.

33

"Something bad, Matt, something bad, boy . . ."

"It's mother!" Matt blurted. "Where is she?"

"She . . . they . . . they were driving downtown . . . a truck . . . it demolished the car. Both my girls . . . gone . . . both my girls . . . *both my girls!*"

And Matt, emotionally frozen, tearless, had been the one to comfort the old man. At the double funeral Matt had spent minutes beside each of the caskets, staring at one and then the other of the two who had been life to him, had been love, had been meaning, had been everything. The worst had come and nothing else, he thought, ever can be this bad—never.

Some instinct in him understood the danger of a grief this massive. He did not permit himself to feel it, nor allow even one tear. He had the sense that the penalty for the loss of control for even a single instant would be destruction.

After his mother's death he continued for a while staying with his oldest uncle and aunt. In the next three or four years living in, but basically outside, all the households of his other relatives, Matt always figuratively turned and walked away from whatever threatened to move him emotionally and soften him. None of the families really wanted him. They had financial problems of their own; he was an extra burden. Withdrawn, suspicious, he was alert to the unsaid things everyone might be feeling. He made himself as inoffensive as possible, but he was not at home with any of them, nor a part of anything but himself. He toughened himself and determined to let nothing bother him.

He began having daydreams that shamed him: somebody would be sick or hurt and he would go to them and be so sorry for them that they'd get well from sympathy. When he was himself he'd sneer, knowing nobody got well from just being looked at softly.

He began shaping the dreams more sensibly: he wouldn't just look into their eyes, he would be a doctor, and know what real medicines to use. His role in the dream had changed, but the feeling of softness while he performed his act was the same. At the end of his dream the person lost all his pain, and then something strange happened. When the patient was well he would not recognize Matt. He— often she—would look into Matt's eyes and see merely what all healthy, happy people saw. Only in a condition of sickness could they look into him and see the depth of understanding and sympathy and feeling.

He tried to reject such fantasies. But in his early teens he realized they *were* a part of him, a soft but true part of him. Maybe the best part of him. He knew somehow, someday, he was going to be a doctor for real.

He thought of himself as a pre-pre-pre-med student before he started high school. Excellent grades were vital and in the next four years he became a grind; money was vital and he scrambled for odd jobs and hoarded every dollar he could since there wasn't anything left of his mother's insurance. He started college on a scholarship and with money in the bank. Besides, he got a 20-hour-a-week job and ended the first year with more money than he'd started with and won another scholarship. During that summer he got a high-paying, production-line factory job in Detroit. The next summer a better one came through in Chicago.

He was doing fine in his third year of college with a movie-usher job, free board and a small, illegal business. The theater was huge. In the past it had housed stage spectacles, but much of it had been closed off. There was space galore in some of the backstage lofts and he not only set up a cot for himself but let in ten other students at a dollar a week. Eventually, the manager caught on, threw them all out and was in the mood to call the police till Matt appealed to his finer sensibilities by giving him all the profits plus twenty dollars.

Nonetheless, he was out of a job. To top if off he got double pneumonia and a semester was lost entirely. He stayed out another full semester, working at good wages and living on as near nothing as he could.

When he was finally an accepted med student he had a sense of exhaustion, at the very time the preliminaries were over and the real battle began. He'd assumed he could hold some kind of a job and get his work done at the same time. Within a month he knew better.

The first-year weed-out process was heavy and anything less than his total effort was dangerous. He thought if he could get through that rough year, absorbing all he had to absorb, he could coast the next year, just enough to leave some time and energy for a job. He was wrong. If anything the demands were greater, and he had to keep up or get dropped. The schoolwork used him up; an outside job was impossible. He began applying for loans, scholarships.

By Christmas nothing had come through. He picked up a little money during that short vacation and marked time and lost weight. The extra pressure had reflected in his grades. He'd slipped into the bottom third of the class. He knew his applications for a loan or scholarship would be considered in conjunction with his current record. Finally one of the loans came through part way, just enough to get him skimpily through another semester.

When summer came he had nothing. He grabbed any job he could get, for a week, a few days, even a day at a time. He barely survived, let alone saved anything.

In late August he was notified to report for steady work in a factory where he'd worked the summer before. The job paid well. He knew that in a year he would have enough to take a try at another year of school. It would mean falling behind, forgetting some of what he'd learned. The ground he'd lose was important, time was important. The factory job was no loaf-through; it would use up his vitality, distract him. The pattern of losing a year, making it up, losing another, would be endless. How long could he endure grim dedication when there was no guarantee? How long could he deprive himself of casual pleasures when there was no end in sight? How much longer could he, with forbidden money in his pocket, be strong enough to turn away from lovely girls because he couldn't afford a date or a gift or an obligation? Not much longer, and if there was no hope ahead of him . . . *no* longer.

The catch-as-catch-can sex in his life left him hungering. Sometimes he yearned himself sick for sweetnesses, for softnesses, for a continuing warmth and beauty, for someone to love—anyone. And if she should come at a lonely time, at a time when he was cut off from the world he'd not yet gained— He turned down the job.

He registered at school with less than twenty dollars to his name. He had nothing for tuition, nothing for books, food, rent. He was helpless. He couldn't do anything but inform the dean of his situation. The time had come for the big question to be asked of his chosen profession. If it thought enough of his record, his potential, him, it would give him a hand. The fact that medicine did reach down and claim him was the greatest thing that had ever happened. It was an estimation of his worth, the sum of all the opinions of all his professors who had helped him.

The internship he got after becoming a for-real M.D. was among the three he'd hoped for. During his first year at the hospital the chief surgeon had taken an interest in him and selected him for specialization. He survived the competition for three years and the chief, Dr. Adatti, suggested that he apply for a surgical residency in that very hospital.

Dr. Adatti had been his god above the gods. He was famous, brilliant, and it was an incomparable privilege to be allowed to scrub with him, to listen, to learn, to observe his flawless technique, to absorb bit by bit pieces of priceless knowledge. A month before the end of his internship, Matt was assured unofficially that he had been accepted as a surgical resident.

Just afterward he was on duty in Emergency late one night when a man came in suffering extreme abdominal distress. Matt diagnosed acute appendicitis and ordered the man prepared for operation. He called the chief surgical resident, also Dr. Adatti.

Waiting, Matt scrubbed with two other interns. Nurses prepared the laparotomy setup; the anesthetist prepared the patient. Neither a resident nor Dr. Adatti had arrived 20 minutes later. Matt watched the clock, began to gnaw his lips. The other interns had agreed on the diagnosis. The surgical resident didn't come. Dr. Adatti was on his way, but Matt felt that every minute counted.

He decided not to wait, to perform the operation himself. He was unauthorized to do it. It was a calculated risk.

He got in, swiftly, and ran into bowel adhesions, hernia and a jungle of bleeders, in addition to a badly inflamed appendix swollen to the rupture point. He excised the appendix. While he was suturing, the wound flooded with blood. The patient went into shock.

Matt swiftly located then clamped the ruptured artery, ligated it. He worked unperturbedly, not taking his eye from the operative field while he gave the proper orders for drugs and infusions to deal with shock. Within minutes the crisis was past; Matt made his closure. The patient was taken to the recovery room. Matt took off his mask and gloves and looked up. Dr. Adatti was staring at him.

37

"You almost lost a patient."

"I can explain—" Matt began.

"Shut up, intern, when you are being spoken to. I know you can explain it. I know you did what you considered necessary. I won't take issue on that. I will even assume that your diagnosis was as accurate as I have come to expect from you. I watched you. You are excellent, Beaumont. You are precise. You are sure. You are bold. And you are swift. In other words, you are a magnificent machine. But you are not a doctor. You are not a surgeon. You will never be a surgeon."

"Excuse me, Dr. Adatti," Matt said, horrified by his tone, his expression. "What are you talking about?"

"Sweat. You didn't sweat. Dane was dripping. Pollard was dripping. You had a patient's life in your hands and it did not trouble you. I have never known any surgeon of merit who failed to sweat. I myself with that responsibility would have lost three pounds in those three minutes. I have made a great mistake about you, Beaumont. I will rectify that mistake. Your residency here will never become official while I am alive. I can't express my contempt for your cold-bloodedness."

"On the contrary, Doctor. You express it well," Matt said hoarsely. "If it's a joke, forgive me. To me, it's not funny, you see. Can you mean you're going to ruin my career because of my nonconformist sweat glands?"

"Dont be funny with me, Beaumont."

"Then, seriously. Because I've spent my life learning to be above and better than my personal emotions, because I've developed a control to the point where I don't exist except for the sake of a patient when I'm on duty . . . can you mean to tell me, Doctor, that a man of your stature . . ." He looked in panic at Dr. Adatti's face, implacably hostile.

"I have told you. You are a machine, not a man, not a human."

"You can damn me like that? You! The man who taught me everything I know! The man I respect above all men can say that to me. No, Dr. Adatti. You *can't* mean it. You *must* know me better than that."

"I'm sorry, Beaumont. That is my judgment."

He turned his back. He walked out.

38

Matt stood dumb-struck, too shocked to move. Suddenly he bent forward and vomited.

For a few days he scrubbed with other surgeons and marked time. It was known that no official action had been taken to block his residency appointment. Fellow interns, residents and older surgeons believed that Adatti would and should relent.

It had been so impossible for him to believe Dr. Adatti had renounced him that Matt decided the attack must have been a kind of final testing. At any time Matt would be called to his office. Dr. Adatti would probe to discover if he fully understood the test's meaning, its necessity in the training of the ideal surgeon who must be above his own pain, know and surmount his own weaknesses. Ending, Dr. Adatti would allow one of those brief, relaxed periods and, smiling, would relate an episode in his own training, when he himself had had to function against the hostility of an admired superior.

The call didn't come. Word came to Matt that he could petition for a hearing and perhaps convince Dr. Adatti that he had been in a comatose or hypnotic state, too scared to know what he'd been doing—which would have been a lie, which would have been admitting that he had been wrong. He had not been wrong. Dr. Adatti had been wrong.

Dr. Adatti was a great man, a good man, but wrong. Matt loved him, but his hero was wrong. He would have done almost anything to be reinstated in his good graces, but he could not go where he was hated, where he was thought to be a monster, where he was not loved, only tolerated—destruction was better than that. If he would use his power against him, so be it. He couldn't lift a hand to save himself. But the time would come, the time would come when Dr. Adatti would know he had been wrong.

The time had passed when he might have obtained another residency for the next year. He finished his internship with nothing except the brief, cold advice from Dr. Adatti to change his specialty.

Matt got a job with a surgical supply house and began applying to good, then mediocre, then poor hospitals. Eventually he got a residency and later he obtained an Army commission as a surgeon. In Korea he broadened his experience and under battlefield conditions learned to endure stress he couldn't have imagined in the hospitals. And the only sweating he did resulted from heat.

Out of uniform he joined the staffs of excellent hospitals in Boston and San Francisco for a year each. He'd come here to Northside General with a good reputation a few years ago and his overall mortality rate through thousands of operations was slightly over three per cent, and during the past several hundred his rate was below two per cent —and he hadn't done it by selecting only the safe, easy ones. He took what came. On the hard ones he came through by a process of pre-worry that involved performing the operations over and over in his mind. Imaginatively, he ran through all the difficulties he was likely to encounter, so that he was ready for them almost every time they showed up in reality.

He supposed he'd run through Judith Chalmer's operation twenty times already, waking at odd times and visualizing intensely some new problem. He'd read everything he could find that was remotely pertinent, including certain monographs and chapters in books by Dr. Adatti, whose death five years ago he still felt as a personal loss second only to his mother's and Aunt Sally-Dee's.

Reaching the phone booth to call the cab to the hospital, he knew he should phone Vicky and assure her there was nothing final about his walking out. She knew she was wrong; to become actually responsible for withholding a chance at full life from Judith Chalmers would be unbearable to Vicky. She had depended on him to bring her safely, tenderly, across to his side. But he had told her to go straight to hell, as if he were some kid—or deficient in love, understanding, or human feeling.

Her phone rang and rang. He began thinking about the night she'd taken her car out on a highway and driven the center line at 120. He knew the emotional excesses she was capable of, the suicidal hysterias. He'd better get back to her! No, he mustn't mistrust her, mustn't cater to her childishness. He must help her strengthen herself. But if she was lying curled on her bed, as he had often seen her, crying her heart out because he had abandoned her—She didn't answer. He'd have to go to her.

He phoned a cab and went out to wait for it. He looked

at his watch and shook his head. He should get to the hospital.

When the cab pulled up he got in quickly. He settled back and then just stared.

The driver peered back at him. "Where to?"

"Take me—" he began. He cleared his throat. "To the hospital, Northside General."

Chapter Four

Matt's thoughts about Vicky began to dissolve automatically, with no effort of his will, when he came within view of Northside General Hospital's handsome, eight-story main building.

He considered Northside General the city's best. Well coordinated by an efficient administration, the chiefs of the services were generally very good men; the diagnostic equipment was modern and, more important, the technicians were dependably excellent. The medical records department was first-rate; the system of consultations, with the requirement of a written opinion from each consultant, forced clear, accurate thinking and better diagnoses. All hospitals respected the principles of aseptic and antiseptic procedure; NSG practiced them too, not only in the operating rooms but in the ward utility rooms and patients' rooms.

He left the cab and went inside. He paused at the physicians' directory panel and flipped the switch that lighted his name there, on repeater boards upstairs and at the telephone switchboard to signify his presence in the hospital.

He crossed the lobby with a kind of detached, pleasant buoyancy. He rode up to the eighth floor and found the surgical ward in a familiar state of mild disorganization due to the Sunday evening influx of visitors.

The hospital people moved imperturbably among the outsiders following their own patterns: nurses and interns in white going in and out of rooms, up and down the broad, pale green corridors on the hushed, dark-green composition floors; student nurses in blue, carrying packs, trays.

Dr. Arleigh Coleman, a brisk, sharp-featured, balding man in a tweedy gray suit hailed him. In his forties, Coleman was one of the visiting staff that contributed to the high rating of NSG's surgical service.

"Hi, Matt."

"Hello, Arly."

42

"I hear," he said, his glance dropping to Matt's brief case, "you finished the endocrine studies."

"Yes. And I'd like another consultation with you, Fred and Chuck on the Judith Chalmers case Wednesday or Thursday."

"I'll set it up. I said it before, I say it again: If that operation could be done you're the man could do it. Hated setting my judgment against yours, Matt. Anxious to confirm you, but—hell." A grimace of pain crossed Arly's face.

"I start your ulcer chewing?" Matt asked.

"No. Party last night. Well, suppose I'll see you in Vera Dell's room around nine, 'Dr. Pygmalion.' "

"Check, 'Dr. Pygmalion.' "

They laughed and went separate ways. Matt walked on toward the nursing station where he saw, among a group of doctors, another and most important "Pygmalion"—Al Horner. Horner, a maxilla-facial surgeon and dermatologist, was chiefly responsible for the reconstruction of Vera Dell's face.

Vera Dell, in her middle twenties, was a hospital employee and had, in fact, worked in Pathology since she finished high school. She had shown ability, and with encouragement of superiors, she'd attended night classes and qualified herself as a technologist by the time she was twenty-two.

She'd proven unusually conscientious, going out of her way to get work done, earning the admiration and respect of people in all the services. She'd achieved a pleasing personality against great odds, and she was well-liked, but unfortunately she inspired neither love nor lust. After an auto collision and botched surgery when she was fourteen, she had limped and her face had been rendered ugly. That an otherwise desirable, healthy girl had been able to sublimate her natural instincts and make such a fine adjustment was considered a kind of miracle.

Then about a year ago she had waylaid an orderly in an empty room and opened her blouse to show her breasts. She'd lifted her skirt to the waist for another intern. There were whispers of more shocking conduct.

The psychiatric services attempted to brainwash her into an acceptance of her lot and for a few months she seemed to be fine. Then one morning she walked out of the rest room wearing a cloth over her face and not another stitch.

She had just stood there stating the silent, naked truth—that her body was neither malformed nor repulsive, that it made demands on life impossible to refuse for the sake of mind, pride, respect.

Matt and his fellows had responded as to any emergency, feeling a keen responsibility. Matt's own contribution had been reasonably simple: orthopedics involving traction of one leg, then surgical freeing and extension of tendons and muscles in hip and lower abdominal areas.

Transplanted rib cartilage helped reshape her nose, a small steel-tube insert corrected her jaw line. A patent fibrous composition substance filled out the line of one cheek. Grafts of her own skin replaced one eyelid and scars on her cheeks, chin and upper throat. When the bandages came off, possibly this week, it should be a lovely face. Matt, his three fellow Pygmalions, as well as most all hospital personnel, were rooting for Vera Dell.

Unfortunately the project had stirred up some moral indignation. The chief moralist in the case was Dr. Amos Dirken, a round, red-faced, white-haired old gentleman as twinkly-eyed as Santa Claus and externally as jovial. He hadn't quite reached the age of retirement and though he was barred from the major operating rooms he still occasionally performed minor surgery, undependably. A lifelong opportunist who'd entrenched himself socially posing as a local Grand Old Man of medicine, he spent much of his time in hospital politics, bringing his weight to bear from above when he was rebuffed on the working level.

Dirken had ridden the crests of all the medical fads, and probably still had jars of leeches and a discredited diathermy machine in his office. His particular favorite operation had been removal of the uterus and ovaries. He never sparkled more brightly than when he was recounting some case of "female trouble" he'd been able to diagnose instantly and "correct" unhesitatingly by this method. It was still his belief that a woman's sexuality somehow stood between her and virtue. Although he hardly dared confess it, Dirken was one of those doctors who approached illness as a kind of visitation of demons and a proof of guilt; in the case of women, sexual guilt.

He had intruded himself into Vera Dell's case and insisted that, her trouble being sexual, her cure was simple: castration. He had plagued Arleigh Coleman and Al Horner

44

repeatedly. Matt had brusquely rebuffed him several times, looking at him as if he wasn't there. But Dirken had barged into his office exuding that sickening, jolly good-fellowship. Without raising his voice Matt had told him precisely and comprehensively what he thought of him.

"To sum this up, Dr. Beaumont," Dirken had said, his smile a trifle de-sweetened, "you hate me."

"In the same sense, Dr. Dirken, that I hate cancer."

"In the same sense that you hate the good! I'm no man's enemy. I have wanted to be your friend. But you reveal yourself, Beaumont. This girl, this Vera Dell, was a good person, useful, serving the highest ideals of mankind, a credit to her sex. She was afflicted and lacked the strength to combat her affliction. The cure is known: the removal of that element of her which drives her away from her higher self. She needs help. But you and the others propose to aggravate her affliction, to give her greater allure which will add to the poor girl's temptation. Oh, it would be a feather in your cap. But what about that poor girl? Shame, sir!"

"Those mush-mouthed rationalizations turn my stomach. Get it in your head, Dirken, we're not going to turn that girl over to you to castrate."

"Castrate!" Dirken went completely out of control. "God damn you! Don't use that word to me again or I'll smash that stone face of yours. Castration! How dare you! How dare you, you filthy, low, vile, ugly, filthy . . ."

"If you're groping for words try some of these I picked up in the Army."

In an emotionless voice he offered a batch of Anglo-Saxon and Oriental profanities and obscenities of a particularly down-to-earth variety, and continued with no change of tone: "Then, if you'll excuse me, I've got some work to do."

Now as Matt got closer to the nurses station he saw Dirken, faced the other way behind Al Horner. Standing back to back almost like duelists about to step off ten paces; Dirken was talking to somebody while Al Horner, smiling obscurely, eavesdropped.

Vera Dell's Number 1 "Pygmalion," Al Horner, was a narrowly tall man who needed only a cape and string tie to look like a poet. Gray and fifty-odd, his face was young; if his joke were true that he retooled it annually, it would have been his best advertisement. He earned high

fees and was often defensive about being a "cosmetic surgeon," but more often he was so vain it was laughable—
unless you saw his results.

He winked at Matt, very slowly, as if fearing to alert
Dirken. But Dirken glanced around, saw Matt, cleared his
throat and bustled off down the corridor.

"Hello, Al. What's he up to?"

"Hi, Matt. He was praising the marvelous work we're
doing on Vera. Blowing our horn for us. Can you believe it?"

"Sure. If you can't lick 'em, join 'em."

"That's it, probably," Al said with a trace of disappointment. "Incidentally, I was talking about Vera to Miss Tanner yesterday and she wants to go to work on her psycho-
logically. She says you agree she should. She's going to be
up here on a case of yours tonight anyway, so she said
she'd come in earlier and see Vera."

"In fact Tanner just got off the elevator," Matt said,
without turning around.

Al Horner's eyes widened. "The man still knows her
step, and him engaged, too. Forgetting the world's sexiest
psychologist isn't so easy."

"It's easy. But, Al, don't mention my knowing her step.
She'd overinterpret; you know these psychologists."

"I'd like to. Excuse me, Matt. Beauty calls." Al went
past him toward her.

Matt glanced around briefly and Elise Tanner, waiting
down by the elevators dressed in a cream-colored suit and
a small, chic hat, gave him a tart grin and wave of the
fingers. Her bright, white face was as fresh as if she'd just
washed it in snow and she looked vaguely unprofessional
with those long smooth legs and sexy black bangs.

She worked in the psychiatric service, and he'd dated her
for a year. When she wasn't bickering, Elise was an easy,
stimulating companion and a smart, cool girl except in bed
where she was passionate to the point of fierceness.

Elise had adored him as a stud. The man she loved and
respected was Dr. Wiedrick, her chief in the psychiatric
service, who had never asked her for a date, let alone made
love to her. She'd told Matt she would refuse Wiedrick if
he wanted her sexually *because she respected him too
much.*

This worship from below and afar of another man was

46

grit enough in Matt's teeth, but he usually shrugged and enjoyed what he had. However, on their final date, one night before he had met Vicky, everything had come to a head. It had been assumed he would take Elise to the hospital fund-raising ball. When pressure had been put on Wiedrick to attend the function, he'd invited Elise. She'd leaped to accept. In trying to explain to Matt the necessity of her choice she'd said that since the affair was official she couldn't be publicly allied with Surgery!

Psychiatry's and Elise's underlying attitude was that all disease was psychogenic in origin and since you couldn't cut an emotional conflict apart with a knife, surgery, while sometimes unavoidable, should be abolished. Or if it must exist it should know its subordinate place. He had never really told her his estimation of *her* specialty. After he did she looked at him as at a blasphemer.

"Kindergarten-level psychology, you say?" she cried. "Shallow? Dr. Wiedrick a hollow drum? Bumbling half-wit dealers in banalities, falsifications, oversimplifications? Uncomprehending label pasters-on? Why, I'm *nothing* like that."

"But you're trying to get down to that level—Wiedrick's level. You know more than that, you're better than that. And to see you admiring a—"

"Who're you to judge? He's got a Master's, a Ph.D., a—"

"Who am I to judge? I've read him, I've heard him lecture. I've read the words of the men who originated the theories and techniques he pretends to honor but doesn't grasp, or else distorts!"

"That's jealousy talking."

"Elise, if you make a hero out of a man you *know* is violating principles you profess to respect, you're not serious about your work."

"Suddenly the great defender of *my* profession."

"Your profession, hell. It's a fragment of what good G.P.'s and surgeons practice automatically—the organism's a whole, mind-body, psycho-soma. Hippocrates spelled it out three thousand years ago. Don't take that superior-knowledge attitude with me."

"Don't think you'll ever sleep with me again."

"After this, can you think I'd want you?"

Elise changed her mind after Vicky came on the scene.

47

Competition inspired her and for a while she badgered him to come to her apartment and prove in bed that he didn't want her any more.

"As a matter of fact," he'd told her only a month ago, "if I felt the slightest need to prove anything, I could get into a bed with you and go to sleep and never touch you."

"Sure, sure, if you didn't touch me and didn't look at my body you'd be fine."

"I could look. I could touch. I could kiss and fondle you; you could fondle me; whatever stimulation you wanted to use I could resist."

"You've got a mule streak; maybe you *could* will your senses not to respond. But, by God, it would take all you've got. Give me that much. Be at least that gentlemanly. I gave you a hell of a lot of pleasure. Admit it. You're a perfect bastard if you don't."

"Admitted."

"For heaven's sake, quit talking like a fool, saying you wouldn't find me desirable again—under the right circumstances, you know you would. Let's face it. You, and I, go for sex like tigers."

"I'm no longer roused by anybody but Vicky, and the reason isn't just her sexual pull."

"Oh, boy," Elise jeered lightly. "Love! Delayed adolescence, darling. You just never had the time or money to indulge in it before; now it caught up to you."

"There you go, oversimplifying. Love's complex, a two-way street. She also loves me—meaning she enjoys me physically *and* she respects and admires and believes in me. That's the extra something, Elise, the something that focuses my total loyalties on Vicky and makes it impossible for another woman to get through to me, no matter how desirable she may be. You especially are no match for Vicky. I wasn't first in everything with you. You held back big, important things that a man values most: respect, pride in me."

"I suppose you'd have preferred my professional esteem to what you got."

"Absolutely."

"Well, let's forget it. You're happy and I'm happy."

She let it hang. She waited for him to ask if she was now giving her all to her honored chief. He wanted to know. He sat and he didn't ask. He watched her hands as she stood up and smoothed her skirt around her hips and

48

found himself remembering her bedroom with its delights boxed in by that God-awful wallpapering of Rorschach ink blots and he looked up at her with a kind of savagery because he could easily imagine her possessed by Wiedrick. And though he had not wanted her he'd not wanted that bastard to have her either.

"Matt," she'd said, grinning. "It takes fewer muscles to smile than to frown."

"But why be lazy?" he said, and grinned in spite of himself. "You're a not entirely unlikable little bitch."

"I'll treasure that. Take care of yourself, Matt."

"You too, Elise."

He'd be seeing Elise later this evening and he didn't feel one way or another about it. He went over the general progress reports on his patients with Miss Shay, taking a few notes. He signed release forms the admitting office had sent up for Mr. Castleton and Mrs. Stulfer, two patients going home tomorrow.

"They were asking if you'd see them tonight," Miss Shay said, "since you'll be busy when they leave in the morning."

"I'll be seeing them."

"Oh, that's fine, Doctor. They'll be glad."

"When I finish with my pre-ops I'll be looking in on the postoperatives and end up on the seventh floor. In case I miss Dr. Fenton," Matt said, referring to the anesthesiologist, "would you tell him I'd like to see him before he goes, Miss Shay?"

"Of course, Dr. Beaumont."

He started toward Room 811 when "his" interns, Hank Simmons and Shep Green came out of the physicians lounge, looking crisply professional in fresh whites.

Each had come from a good medical school and had shown unusual poise as a general intern. Matt had been influential in their choosing surgery and since then he'd had a major role in their training. They scrubbed with him as first and second assistants on most of his operations and inevitably a bond had grown between them.

Shep Green, in his next-to-last year of surgical internship, was a vital, stocky young man with a broad, ingratiating face, a clear, quick intelligence and a vast, unruly impatience. Learning a standard technique or procedure he set about devising variations; it was not enough for him to diagnose correctly from simple, clear-cut symptoms; he

49

searched for new interpretations, rare diseases. Matt liked his speculative bent and only curbed him when he tried to push ahead of his actual competence. Shep felt ready not only to stand as first assistant but in Matt's place at the operating table. In fact, in an emergency he'd be readier to take over than Hank, even though he knew less and probably had smaller potential ability.

Hank Simmons, a tall, moodily handsome fellow with warm, deep-set eyes, was in his final year of internship. A good diagnostician, his physical examination of patients was marked by a good touch, knowing but gentle when sensitive areas were involved. His manual dexterity and mechanical skill were considerable and even with the patient fully anesthetized he handled the living tissue with respect, as though he knew, even without Matt's lectures on the subject, the necessity for minimizing the traumatic violence. But the point at which Hank's virtues might become excessive was tricky. His admirable distaste for causing injury or pain could degenerate into the inability to do it for whatever purpose.

Somehow, the closer Hank came to the time when he must undertake full responsibility, the more he shrank. He couldn't be blood-shy after hundreds of operations. During them he not only looked, listened, answered questions and learned everything he should know, but participated, wielding forceps and needles, ligaturing arteries, suturing organs, tissues, fascia, muscle, skin. He had undertaken arterial shunts, nerve transplants, resections; he could do parts of the whole in almost everything, but always within the framework of Matt's overall responsibility. It was correct that Hank do only what it was safe to entrust him with and only as it was assigned to him.

On the other hand, he had not yet asked to make an opening incision and he'd never made one. Although he was fully capable of standing in Matt's place in a number of standard operations and assuming full responsibility from opening to closure, he hadn't pressed for a chance. Matt had been careful not to rush Hank, but he wondered if he hadn't been over-cautious, unwittingly encouraging dependence in him.

"Good evening, Dr. Beaumont . . . Hello, Dr. Beaumont," they said.

"Hank . . . Shep . . ." he said, nodding to each, his expression amiable but not uncritical. "What do you want?"

"Well," Shep said, "you never invite us to go with you on your eve-of-operations visits; so we kind of thought we'd invite ourselves. O.K.?"

"No," Matt said good-naturedly. "I'll see you as planned when I'm ready to visit the postoperatives."

"But, Dr. Beaumont . . ." Hank said as Matt was about to go.

"This was your idea?" Matt stopped. "Well, what's your reasoning."

"The merit of an idea," Shep said, "should be independent of its source, scientifically speaking."

"Yes, but in this case it's not the idea but the impulse behind it that matters to me. Hank's wanting greater involvement and responsibility is more important than yours, because in less than a year he'll be out of internship and into a residency somewhere. There's no time problem with you. All right, Hank, make it brief."

"I'll try. I've heard postoperative patients speak of you with something more than the high regard expected toward a surgeon who's responsible for his or her improved health. In some instances they've confided that your visit on the eve of operation gave them a special feeling for you. You've spoken of the importance of the eve-of-operation visit and its tremendous psychological value in helping them through the operation. But I don't know your technique."

"It's unteachable. It's hard to explain; but it's a very private matter, a personalization. The proper mood would evaporate with an audience, especially if I have to be aware of myself as a teacher. This is a time when I have to be totally focused on the patient. Sorry I can't help you. I will do this, however: since you've seen the patients a number of times and they know you both, you can go in with me, but only briefly. Let's go."

A few paces along the corridor Hank worried aloud. "Could you refer to the texts you used? The description of the technique might be sufficient."

"There's no technique, no formula to fit all cases. You base your approach on many factors. You master your surgical problem and everything else falls into line. Sometimes it turns out that you get a secondary gain: the patient likes you. That's fine, but irrelevant."

"I'd find that my chief compensation."

"What are you arguing with Dr. Beaumont for?" Shep said disgustedly. "He told you if you know your job as a surgeon and make yourself worth anyone's liking you, they will like you. If they don't, so what? If you were in medicine just to give yourself the nice cozy feeling of being liked you'd set up a general practice, have continuing relationships, like going steady with all your patients all their lives. The surgeon steps into the picture only in a crisis. Then he pinch-hits and gets cheered for a while if he's good; then the patient forgets him. A man that wants to be a surgeon has got no right to look for personal liking from patients as his chief compensation."

"I happen to like people," Hank said defensively.

"That's sweet."

"Another time," Matt cautioned them, "another place. You go on ahead, Hank. We'll catch up in a minute . . . Shep, what the hell!"

"Sorry, Dr. Beaumont," Shep said. "But, frankly, his snide remarks on surgery lately have been getting under my skin. He's becoming a sensitive soul to the point he thinks manly toughness is a crime. He's trying to undermine me and you, too, and it's interfering with my training. I wish you'd do something about him!"

"I will. I guess Hank's got the stuff, but—you know!"

"I know. I'll straighten him out. But not just now. Come along."

He liked his patients and they knew it and were glad to see him—from homely, old Mr. Davis to pretty, young Miss Ruedney. He'd made himself known to them in numerous previous discussions here and in his office, often in conference with close relatives and their family physician. He'd told them, when the operation was finally decided upon, just what, in lay terms, he was going to do and why and what benefits could be expected, what complications were possible. He had no trouble in proving he believed in the operations since he wouldn't have undertaken them otherwise. He never answered their questions offhandedly or condescendingly.

On the one hand, he built confidence and explained why some fears were groundless; on the other, he discouraged them from imagining a session on the operating table was a casual fun affair.

Major surgery, and often minor, too, produced a certain amount of shock to the system, physically and emotionally. To lead a patient on under a false impression was to subject him to stress he wasn't prepared for. Fear was nature's way of preparing the system to sustain shock, and Matt encouraged sensible worry as a part of pre-operative care as important as medication and fortified diets.

Now, within a dozen or so hours of the operation they were conditioned as much as possible in every way. Presently they'd be given a final aid, drugs to guarantee a good night's sleep.

Entering each room with Hank and Shep, he took a look at the chart, spoke as briefly as possible with visiting relatives or, in two cases, attending physicians. Then, alone, he drew up a chair to the bedside. Unlike some of his colleagues, his patients didn't know he had no bedside manner; nor did they judge his face an inexpressive surgical mask. They could see through it. Sometimes he didn't speak first but looked at them receptively, and what was on their minds came out freely.

More often he spoke first. Sometimes it was a simple "Are you going to be all right?" Frequently he began: "If there's anything bothering you, tell me now." In most cases they told him freely. When he had to ask a patient: "You don't think you'll make it, do you?" he had a problem. Usually he solved it right then; in a few instances he'd postponed the operation.

Occasionally he ran into a really insidious attitude where he might have asked: "You don't intend to make it, do you? You don't want to. I'm your suicide weapon." When this element—the Freudians called it the death wish—was there it seemed to override everything. However good the prognosis, however grimly the surgeons and whole medical staff might fight, the patient failed to respond or built minor complications into fatality. Matt and every surgeon dreaded such cases. Fortunately he had none of these tonight. Two of them, however, were overly anxious. How he coped with them, he tried to grasp even as he did it, thinking there might be something basic he could pass on to Hank and Shep. It evaded him.

It was impossible to communicate any of it to Hank or Shep. But he tried when they all stopped for a smoke in the lounge before proceeding to the postoperative patients.

"My role in relationship to you, Hank," he said, "is that

of teacher to student, master to apprentice. In that respect I'm in command of and above the situation. In my relationship to those patients I step down to the patient's level of helplessness, in a sense, and establish what I suppose you'd call rapport or empathy. To some extent I feel their feelings."

Hank gaped at him, uncomprehendingly.

"Is that so hard to grasp?"

"No, but . . ." he said. He left unsaid: "I can't connect it with you."

Matt shrugged, glanced at the doorway as Dr. Fenton, the anesthesiologist, came in, saying belligerently:

"You wanted to see me, Dr. Beaumont?"

"I did, Dr. Fenton."

Bruce Fenton, a former practicing M.D. and now NSG's top anesthesiologist, was scarcely five feet tall. His body was normal but, as he blithely put it, he'd developed his head instead of his legs. Proud of his skill he bristled when questioned about his choice of anesthetics and drugs in any given case. He approached Matt suspiciously.

"Anything special?"

"It's about Mrs. Metzger."

"Yes, what about her? No heart history; but a suspicion of cardiac irritability shows on her chart since she's been in the hospital, putting us in danger of heart arrhythmia under anesthetic. Considering the irritability could lead to asystole or fibrillation, cyclopropane doesn't look so good. So I'm swinging to ether as my major."

Matt turned up a palm and grinned. "You leave me with nothing to say. That was it, Bruce."

"Never will learn to trust me, will you? Well, future surgeons of America," he said, looking at Shep and Hank, "take a leaf from his book. You're not always going to have a Dr. Bruce Fenton to lean on. Say, Matt," he said, his humor noticeably improved, "know that pretty thing in eight-forty-one, Dorothy Ruedney? From what she's heard about you she's afraid that she'll come out of the operating room pregnant."

"What'd you tell her?"

"I said, 'Don't worry, he's a good Joe, he'll abort you free.' "

Matt laughed with him and the others.

"I fixed you up this afternoon, too, Bruce," Matt said.

54

"Remember that jugular fistula case two months ago, the gorgeous blonde, Catherine Norstadt? Seems she wasn't unconscious after all when you had her in the recovery room. Now she's pregnant and hysterical. I did the only thing I could. Told her you'd had your prostate removed and consequently backfired into your bladder. But I worried how we'll convince the court of your innocence. Then it came to me! So, I've got you scheduled for operation Tuesday—a prostatectomy, perineal or suprapubic, take your choice. It's the only way out."

"There's another way out." Bruce laughed. "That door. Good night, Matt. Hank . . . Shep . . . see you in the morning."

Matt looked at his watch. "Lets go see Mrs. Forrest."

Mrs. Forrest, the plump, anxious little woman in the bed had a drainage tube leading from the upper right quadrant of her abdomen to a jar concealed by a paper covering. Matt, Hank and Shep greeted her, then focused their attention on her chart. She'd been on Friday's operating schedule, listed as a cholecystostomy, a drainage of the gall bladder.

In reality, the operation had been a simple one. She'd had all the trappings of a major operation, including going to the operating room and a five-minute general anesthetic. He'd cut the skin and put sutures on the "incision line," attached a tube and bandages and sent her back to her room. Her postoperative recovery pattern had been almost a textbook case.

When they got back to the eighth floor, young Boyer, a junior resident, approached diffidently.

"The chief resident was wondering, Dr. Beaumont, if you can spare them," he said, meaning Hank and Shep.

"Yes. But they've got to have their sack time; they're working with me in the morning."

"We know, sir. It'll only be for an hour or so."

"All right. G'night, Hank . . . Shep."

The floor was clear of visitors as Matt made his way back through several corridors which were quietly alive with orderlies, aides, interns, nurses on the move. Some doors were shut, others gave glimpses of bed preparation activity.

Nearing Vera Dell's room he had a buoyant sense of pleasure about seeing her, or at least her eyes through the pressure bandages on her face. When he turned into her corridor and saw Dr. Amos Dirken with his three fellow Pygmalions outside her closed door he slowed, immediately alert. Al Horner was talking amiably with Dirken. Arly Coleman stood a little distance away with Dr. George Cape.

Arly and George saw Matt and at once moved toward him as if to head him off. George Cape, a ruggedly built man with a lumbering gait and a normally vague air of doom about his strong, deeply lined face, was, like himself, a Fellow of the American College of Surgeons. In Matt's opinion he was the most dependable man at NSG. His habit of concentrated listening seemed to have cocked his head permanently to one side; he spoke so seldom he gave an impression of being tongue-tied. Far from it, he could talk like lightning. He had the enviable ability to dictate descriptions of his operations right in the operating room while he worked, producing reports that were accurate, vivid classics. George Cape had daughters near Vera Dell's age and was emotionally involved in her welfare.

"What's wrong?" Matt said. "Why's her door closed? What's Dirken doing here?"

"The child's depressed and upset," Cape said. "Miss Tanner's in with her. Now, to complicate it, Dirken's horning in."

"Hornering in, you mean," Arly snapped. "Al's certain her face is going to be his masterpiece and that he's outdone himself because it's a labor of love. Dirken plays on his vanity. He wants to see the unveiling."

"Dirken's idea is to divide and conquer," George Cape grumbled. "Turn Al against us if we object."

"So we can't object," Matt decided. "Why play his game?"

George and Arly exchanged relieved glances.

"Well, if it's not going to bother you, Matt, that simplifies it."

"I wouldn't let that politician put me in the position of a heel, depriving Al of a kick. It's mainly Al's show."

"It's not just Al's vanity," Arly put in. "He feels the success will be rubbing Dirken's nose in it."

"Maybe I'd better pass up seeing Vera," Matt said.

"It might be better," George Cape said. "She's got herself in a state over the prospects of the new life. She's worried, too, about her face. It might not come up to Al's hopes—or, in a way just as frightening to her, maybe she *will* be a beauty, and with no experience at it. We've se-

56

dated her. Miss Tanner is staying till she goes to sleep. Miss Tanner did leave word she wants to see you about the Forrest woman, a really fascinating case. You ought to publish that one, Matt."

"It's unilkely. Well, good night. I'll wait for Elise up in the public room."

Chapter Five

Waiting restlessly in the eighth floor public room for Elise, Matt used the pay phone to call Vicky. She didn't answer. He tried again in five minutes. Nothing. He waited out in the hall, chatting briefly with five or six colleagues while they waited for the elevator.

As they went, one after another to families, homes, women who loved them, he felt more and more depressed. He called Vicky again. He tried reaching her at the club, at her parents' home. Then again he phoned her apartment.

While he was counting the fifteenth unanswered ring Elise Tanner, looking fresh-faced and smart in the creamy suit and chic little hat came in. She stood in profile to him, one trim foot half-stepped forward so that her skirt draped itself along the rising flare of her thigh and the curve of her shapely bottom.

When he hung up the phone on the thirtieth ring, Elise walked over to a settee and sat down at one end, crossing her ankles and displaying her long elegant legs, her skirt to her knees.

"Consultation, doctor?" she said tartly, her alert black eyes watching him steadily. "Aren't you going to sit down?"

He shrugged, sat at the other end and took out a pack of cigarettes.

"Me, too." Elise said with a little smile. As he offered the pack she left her hands on her lap and pushed her face toward him, her lips semi-pursed, to receive the cigarette, her eyes closing. Her lashes, as black as her bangs, lay like lacework, lovely against the whiteness of her cheeks. In the past this picture of yielding feminine grace had enchanted him. Often instead of giving her the cigarette he had kissed her. Now, he did neither. He lit his cigarette.

"Oh, you slob," she said, opening her eyes. She reached for his cigarettes, took one, opened her purse to get matches and lit for herself.

"Anyhow, Matt, I'm pleased with you on all counts to-night. You swing to psychosurgery in the Forrest case—"

"Psychosurgery! Don't start that, Elise."

She looked at him challengingly, then shrugged and said rapidly: "All right, seriously—I'd like to have your views on it. Did her need to be operated on amount to a desire to be violated sexually and have the unconscious meaning of marital infidelity? Or is the worry and expense she's causing her husband a disguised attack on him? Or did the 'operation' express a hidden wish on her part to be punished for past guilts, real or imagined? Or might it have been punishment for a crime she contemplates in the future? Or—"

"Or is she," Mat wedged in, "a simple woman who builds complexities to give a larger meaning to her life?"

"Good point. Considering her children are grown and gone, her sense of uselessness and fear of approaching menopause would exaggerate and complicate any other latent tendencies . . ."

For ten or fifteen minutes they exchanged views, theories, speculations in a way he found stimulating. And her approach to Vera Dell was, Matt believed, acutely intelligent. He was scarcely aware that she was swinging the mood to personal involvement when she began to blast Dr. Amos Dirken.

". . . and he wants not only Vera Dell destroyed, he's after you, too. But you're too smart and strong for him!"

Her hand was on his, soft as velvet, and her fingertips moved slightly like an intimate kind of telegraphy, and unconsciously she jiggled one leg, something she always did when she was sexually aroused. The clear directness of her black eyes, the intentness of her focus on him, her overall attractiveness, and most of all his past knowledge of her passionate body in bed worked on him physically before his mind was aware of anything happening.

Suddenly they were looking at one another in one of those heavy, deep-probing silences. Elise moistened her lips, blinked her eyes and drew a deep breath.

"Matt," she said huskily, "I'm so damned lonesome for you. How about taking me home?"

He stood up, shaking his head. "I've got a date!"

"Come for a few minutes." She got up, put her hand in

his and gripped fiercely, gazing up at him urgently. "We'll have coffee, or a beer. I'm not a bad gal, Matt."

"I know, Elise. I know. It's impossible, though. See you tomorrow." He walked out and picked up his car.

He drove to his own cramped apartment and phoned Vicky from there, aching for her. Still no answer. He went back out to his car, deciding to go to her apartment. She'd be there; she'd *have* to let him in.

En route, he passed the hospital again, and knew he was not going to go scratching like a dog on Vicky's door to be let in, not under the conditions she might exact. He parked near the hospital and went in a restaurant he occasionally used.

He was about to have coffee at the counter when in the shadows of a back booth he saw the faintly luminous glow of a woman's face as beautiful as a glimpse of perfection. It seemed to exist alone and this dreamlike impression persisted even while he objectively noted the causes: a booth partition cutting off view of her body, a scarf obscuring her throat. In a moment he realized it was Constanza Vassily. She didn't see him.

Turning to his coffee he wondered at the optical illusion that had made her seem beautiful, but it was idle speculation. His interest in and curiosity about everything was shut out by thoughts of Vicky.

He looked at the clock—quarter to ten. He'd phone at ten. She'd answer and everything would be all right. Nothing final had happened—he couldn't survive a "Vickyectomy."

He'd buy her a present, he thought, rallying. But the candy shop she liked was closed. There was a big all-night drugstore nearby, but she was particular about perfumes; her cosmetics were special blends; she had enough real jewelry to rule out most ornamental trinkets; even her stockings came from a special lingerie shop. Well, tomorrow he'd search around for something to please her, something unique and worthy of her.

The trouble with even a temporary separation was that it would give her time to think about him, look at him objectively. And, he suddenly knew, he couldn't bear close personal scrutiny. Detached from his work, what was he, what had he ever been? He'd known from the time he was a distasteful, cowardly small boy that something was wrong

60

with him, something that made him unworthy. Not all the love, pity and good intentions of his closest relatives had made him really an acceptable part of their homes.

He had a flash image of two faces: his mother's, his aunt's—dead. He felt the sudden acute stabbing sensation of a phantom knife in his heart and his hands trembled and he felt ugly and monstrous, a repulsive creature who could lose everything he loved without tears.

Vicky suspected. Her original sketch of him had shown the strong man in command. Progressively her sketches had penetrated to reveal softnesses, and she liked none of them as well as the first. She'd pointed out that he was unusually nervous when it came to the problem of their home. She sensed or already knew fully how vital that was to a part of him—not to the man she knew and respected and wanted, but to the sniveling, weak, contemptible small boy.

She knew the element of surrender in him, the need to please her, to earn her approval, to surround himself securely with the sweetness of her love. . .

It wasn't, he rationalized, that Vicky was now asking him to prove his love by laying a human head at her feet. After all, Judith Chalmers wouldn't die if he left her alone. In fact, she might if he went ahead. Men he respected were afraid of the operation. Vicky had a right to fear that failure would ruin his and her own future. All Vicky was asking was that he not make a human sacrifice of *her*, not if he truly loved her.

His confidence in himself and the operation might or might not be justified. He got up to pay his check. The only thing he knew for certain was that he was miserable. And so was Constanza Vassily, evidently, he noticed when he glanced back at her booth.

Or, not exactly miserable, but somehow forlorn. Maybe that lonely, forlorn look was what had involved his feelings and made her seem beautiful a few minutes ago. He might be partly responsible for her mood; he'd let her in for that clash with Vicky this afternoon. Then he'd spoken abruptly to her and practically kicked her out of the lab with no thought about how upset she'd been, how she was feeling when she went off alone. No way to treat someone who'd worked as conscientiously for him as she had.

True, he'd given her a bonus, but money didn't count much with a girl like this. She'd been working too hard;

tonight she should have been enjoying things. There was a kind of outrage about a nice girl like Constanza being unhappy and alone when there were so many fine young fellows around. Hank and Shep, for instance, didn't have steady girls. Hank especially would appreciate her and she'd admire his basic dedication to his work, his abilities and warmth. Worth-while girls of her sort had a lot to give a man; Constanza's sympathy and encouragement might do wonders for Hank's confidence if he could win her—the big IF . . . He had to laugh at himself: just when his own love life was delicately balanced between disaster and farce he was ready to fly forth as Cupid! Anyway he'd go back and say hello.

She turned and saw him, and her features, which had been as immobile as a portrait, seemed to flow with warm life.

"How's my friend, Constanza Vassily?"

"Why, hello, Dr. Beaumont. She's fine . . . a little mopey. How're you?"

"A little mopey. Mind if I sit down?"

She smiled and shook her head, and he settled on the seat across from her. There was an unrushed quality about her that made her easy to be with. For a few moments he just sat looking at her fondly. He wondered why Vicky had called her "ballerina-faced."

The dark hair was center-parted and drawn sleekly back from the temples; the forehead was low; the full cheeks broad and high; the eyes glowingly large and solemn. A Slavic face, he guessed, suggesting a certain quiet depth and intensity, a warmth, a . . . well . . . femaleness. The dark-blue gauzy scarf at her throat and matching velvet band across the crown of her head set off her pale, olive-tinted skin.

Though it was like a million pretty faces it had a few uncommonly winsome touches of its own—for instance the curve of her eyelids and the particular way the corners of her. eyes merged with the beginning swell of her soft cheeks. The eyelids lowered; he detected the wispiest of frowns and knew he'd been staring. He said casually:

"How about another sandwich? A dessert?" He looked at the empty dishes and tea pot on the table. "Or tea?"

"That. Yes."

"Think I will, too," Matt said, looking around to find the

waitress. After they'd ordered he said: "I'm sorry about this afternoon; I hope it didn't ruin your evening."

"No," she said faintly. "But I was in a mood. So I went downtown to a movie, a sad movie. You'd think I'd have had sense enough to choose something gay, but oh, no, not me. You know, Dr. Beaumont, I can't stand the kind of person who lets herself be carried down and down and who revels in depressions instead of trying to rally. But I do it." She hunched her shoulders. "It's morbid. Don't you think?"

" 'Physician, heal thyself,' " he said, smiling at her. "Constanza, gland experimenter, look at your glands. The fight situation in the lab this afternoon stimulated your adrenals to overproduce. Your whole system was geared for emergency. You didn't work off the excessive secretions with strenuous action. So they had to be eliminated more slowly; meantime your imbalanced condition causes or intensifies depression."

He went on, elaborating on things she already knew, but she listened as if every word were new and significant. As he talked to her he was again aware of that unrushed quality of hers like a slow, silent inner rhythm. Looking at Constanza's quietly lovely face and meeting the gentle gaze of her eyes, he realized that hers was the unassertive, passive force of a flower.

"As you know, not only the adrenals are involved. . . ." He was glad the waitress arrived. He was getting into quicksand. Both she and he knew the gonads, the sex glands, were important factors.

"I should have reasoned it out," she said. She busied herself with tea bags and hot water, attending not only to her own but his, also. "You like yours strong?"

"No. Very pale. As close to non-tea as possible."

"I love tea," she said, smiling to herself. She poured for him then added his tea bag to her pot and waited. "I suppose it's the Russian and Polish in me, plus the fact I lived nearly eight years in England."

"I didn't know that."

"Yes. My first eight. My father was part of the Polish government in exile in London during World War II. He was killed in the blitz when I was three. My mother's American but we stayed on in England till 1947. I still have traces of a British accent."

"Come to think of it, you do. Nice, too."

"Thank you." She smiled and poured her tea, black as coffee. "Mother came home to Philadelphia and became an R.N. She worked in hospitals there and New Orleans and Baltimore and Chicago and oh, several places, till we came here. Through my school days hospitals were part of my landscape; it never occurred to me to work in any other field. I thought I'd be a nurse, too. But I was good in biology and chemistry in high school, so we decided I should train for lab work. And . . . here I am."

He laughed. "A fast trip! Mother still nursing? I don't think I know her, do I?"

"No. She married a G.P. in Dallas. And the most marvelous thing happened. I've got a year-old baby sister who's just adorable. It makes me so happy. She wanted a baby so much. But while I was growing up she wouldn't even think of remarrying. You see, Mother first married when she was very young, sixteen—it was wartime, you know—so she's not old at all and awfully attractive. Still she wouldn't do a thing about her life till I was set. In my teens I worried that the right man wouldn't come along and she might get too old to have another baby.

"Mother and I got along . . . somehow we didn't have the standard mother-daughter clashes. She said that was the only advantage she knew in not having a father around the house for me. If there'd been one I'd have wanted to be his favorite female. Mother was tough when she had to be, and being a nurse she knew the facts of life and she didn't hold them back from me. She gave me an attitude about morality that I'll always live by . . ."

She began to laugh quietly. "Dr. Beaumont, are you hypnotizing me? Or what's making me give out the life and times of Constanza Vassily? Why, it's terrible of me. You don't have enough on your mind!"

"I'm glad you feel like talking to me. Still, I suppose we should leave your private code of morality alone."

She looked embarrassed. She drank some of her tea, leaving a pink curve of lipstick on the cup. She put the cup down and stared into it.

"Listen," she said hoarsely. "All those weeks in the lab, working with you, I was innocent. Then, this afternoon when our working together was all over, I didn't want to go. I wasn't innocent. I wanted you to like me personally. When I kissed you I wished you would kiss me passionately. After the fight I knew how instinctively right Miss Lassiter had been. And I couldn't bear myself." She raised her eyes unhappily to his, then lowered them. "I was about to tell you the morality code I want to live by. First, honesty with myself. But I was false. I kept myself in ignorance of my real motives. If I'd faced my actual sexual desires I could still feel true to myself."

She suddenly stared at him in a kind of horror. "I'm doing something shabby *right now*. This very minute I'm knifing her in the back. I'm wanting you to want me more than you want her. I know it's futile, but it's so."

"You're straight, Constanza. And now that we have it out, and we both know the situation's impossible, we can handle it. You mustn't let yourself think seriously about me."

"I'm not in love with you," she assured him. "But—I'd better not say it."

"Don't you have a man, Constanza? You need one."

"I have a man. I know my needs. Why I still want you I'm not sure. It may be competitiveness; but I've never been that way, going after somebody because another girl's got him. Whatever it is, I want you to know I feel very badly about it. It's the last thing I want to do—cause you any sort of worry or trouble. If I've already caused trouble between you and Miss Lassiter, I'm sorry—genuinely, Dr. Beaumont. I'm going to get over this. Don't imagine I'll be a problem. I won't. I promise you," she said, her eyes glowing with earnestness.

"I believe you." He smiled at her. "Now, if you'll give me the other check I'll pay them both and I'll go." He glanced at her, then said, "No, I think I'd better take you home."

"I'll be all right."

"At this time of night I'd better take you."

"Well . . ." She put on her jacket and followed him moodily.

"I've got a phone call to make," he told her at the cashier's desk. "It'll only take a minute."

He went into the booth and dialed Vicky's number. She answered in the middle of the first ring. He grinned widely.

"Matt?"

"Yes, darling."

"I've been phoning your apartment. Say you love me. Say you forgive me."

"I do. I do. I'm coming right out."

"Instead of here, would you meet me in Waverly Hills? At *our* house?"

"Now? This late? Well—all right."

"Good," she said excitedly. "where are you?"

"Across from the hospital."

"You start in ten minutes. Let me get there a little before you. I love you. I can't wait."

"Don't go racing, Vicky," he said, but she'd hung up.

When Matt reached the three-acre building site in Waverly Hills the watchman came out of the little shed at the front of the property.

"Evening, Doctor. The Mrs. just got here. I lent her a flashlight and she's up to the house now."

"Well, thanks. That'll be a help."

The as-yet-unpaved driveway penetrated fifty yards of woods and emerged into a spacious area dotted with stacks of lumber, brick, pipe, cement sacks, sand piles and assorted work paraphernalia. Later the clearing would become lawns, pool and patio.

There was enough light from the night sky to show the nearly completed structure clearly. It "walked up the hill" in three levels, its decks and walls forming a sturdy, angular pattern; its materials of fieldstone, timber, dark and light brick, glass brick and glass sheets gave the design variety and smartness.

Above, he could see Vicky's white car and a moving flashlight in the master bedroom. He followed the rutty road's circling climb and parked beside her car. The air was mild, slightly moist, and there was a breeze, sounding like a hoarse whisper through the foliage. He liked the feel of quiet space and privacy.

"Vicky," he called, walking over to the deck and down toward the open sliding glass door of the master bedroom. "Vicky."

"Coming, darling, coming!"

She followed the words immediately, rushing in the wake of the down-slanting flash beam. A fur coat swung like a dark bell around her slight body and her quick slim legs, encased to mid-calf in tight red pants, flashed with motion; she seemed to spring along on masses of foam, her bare feet ankle-deep in white fur slippers.

For several moments he just held her, his cheek against her hair.

The flashlight clunked on the planks and she opened her fur coat and pressed herself snugly against him so that he could feel the contours of her body, warm against him.

She lifted her face to him, closing her eyes. In full light her mouth was like ripe tropical fruit, in the dimness that now obscured the rest of her features, it stood out, a dark richness which drew him blindly.

He kissed her, his lips sinking into the softness and he kissed her again and again, lingeringly, savoring her feminine sweetness. His hands moved upward against the hairs of her fur coat into the infinitely more voluptuous silky mass of her hair. The pliant softness of her body against his made him pleasurably aware of his size, his strength to protect the precious delicacy of her. So tender was his mood that the thought of anything hurting her was intolerable, including even male sexual aggression.

"I love you, Matt. We're never going to fight again." She kissed him several times, quick, light impressions of her lips, then freed herself and retrieved the flashlight. "Come and let me show you something."

The walls of the vast, master bedroom were plastered, the mirror panels already in place between the floor-to-ceiling windows on three sides; the floor was unfinished but laid. Vicky aimed the flashlight at the center of the floor where she had spread, side by side, two large satin quilts, one pink, one blue. He blinked in surprise, then grinned across his shoulder at her, but she was peering at him gravely.

"This is our home, Matt," she said, her voice low and intense. "Our future. It's the one thing totally new in both our lives, totally disconnected with our pasts. I want to bind us to it and make it really ours, our own world, a true part of our love, our hearts, our bodies. I want to infuse this empty house with meaning; I want to make it real to us, to our future. Love me here, Matt. Now. Let me give you my love. Now, lover, husband . . ."

He was so powerfully touched he couldn't speak. He marveled at her, feeling the truth of her instinct. Once again he felt incredibly privileged to possess her; he was abruptly glad he'd known emotional pain in the past or he could not have appreciated the happiness Vicky gave him.

She turned off the flashlight and moved away. Presently his eyes adjusted to the darkness. Vicky stood by the quilts, as at the edge of a satin sea, and dropping her satin coat and removing the fur slippers, she stepped in barefoot.

She was wearing only a narrow band across her breasts and the tight red pants. Moving to the edge of the quilt he saw that the pants were cut very low, the tops following a shallow, curved line across her bare stomach, inches below her small, oval navel.

Dimly in the three mirror panels he could see her exquisite body reflected from each side and in back. He reached out and lay his palm against her soft belly and stroked her flesh gently. Then dropping to one knee and embedding his hands in the upper swelling of her hips, he pressed his cheek to her belly, then his full face.

He kissed, and then opening his lips, he flicked her belly with his tongue and felt the quick little spasm of pleasure run through her and heard her catch her breath. With sudden feverishness he began to kiss her delicious body all over, turning her completely around and moving up her back to her shoulders and neck and then, pulling the band from her breasts he kissed and sucked her nipples.

She lay on her back, quivering and breathing rapidly. Her hands clutched his head, pressing him to her, and when, crouching over her, he kissed her mouth fiercely, she whimpered with pleasure. She arched herself up and down while her hands were frantically pushing the pants down off her hips.

When he moved away to get out of his clothes, she crawled after him and wound her arms around him, kissing his face and mouth passionately. She had the red pants off her hips, halfway down her thighs and he pulled them the rest of the way and as he was freeing her feet he kissed them.

He moved between her knees and she arched her pelvis, yielding her body to him. When he caught her buttocks firmly in his grasp and drew her to him she reached down to touch him, guide him. His whole body was tense as he thrust, entering her with a sensation of pure bliss.

He was aware then of lowering his upper body to hers and feeling her breasts mash under him as her arms locked around his back. He was aware of the passionate outflow of her words in his ear, loving words, sweet words. But mostly

68

he was aware of their rhythm, the supple wavelike rising, rolling motion of their fused bodies, the exquisite heat of her intimate female flesh embracing and containing and giving joy to his maleness. *My woman! My Mate! The sweetness of my existence!* As he felt, and Vicky's tensing, vibrant body felt, the quickening tempo, the approach to climax and ecstasy, there was a moment's regret, a swift brief knowledge of loss. And then, climax, and with it a sense of complete happiness.

"I love you, Vicky. I love you!"

Chapter Six

His first operation, a nephropexy, was scheduled for 7:30. The anchoring of a mobile right kidney was simple, but the patient was Mrs. Metzger, with the cardiac irritability problem. Though Bruce Fenton was competently aware of the danger, the specter of fibrillation haunted Matt as he entered the 8th floor surgeon's dressing room at 6:50.

There were a score of doctors in the lounge and locker room, operating and assisting surgeons on the morning schedule, a couple of attending physicians there to observe. He went directly to his own locker, his nods and greetings terse, his mood withdrawn. He changed into white ducks, sleeveless blouse, comfortable soft-soled canvas shoes, and finished his cigarette.

He went out and checked in at the operating room supervisor's desk. Then he went along the wide quiet corridors in the suite of major and minor operating rooms to Major Operating Room A. He by-passed the scrub room and went through the swinging doors of the patients' entrance.

The big twenty-square-foot, soundproofed, air-conditioned room was dominated by the empty operating table with its adjustment wheels and levers on a solid pedestal in the center under the big, unlighted white cone of the powerful, glareless lamp.

Hank and Shep were waiting for him, watching Dr. Fenton and an assistant at the anesthetic machine. An orderly and a blue-uniformed student nurse were assisting the masked, white-uniformed circulating nurse and the green-gowned, masked and gloved instrument nurse set up sterilized instrument and supply tables.

They paused to greet him. Dr. Fenton nodded, returned to his gauges and cylinders. Matt spoke to them all, then paused near the scrub nurse laying out orderly lines of gleaming stainless steel forceps, clamps, hemostats, needles, needle holders, knives, knife blades, handles, pronged and smooth blade retractors, blunt and pointed dissectors. Her pads, compresses, sterile towels, bandages, tapes and tubes were already in place. Unscrubbed, he kept his distance, checking her needle supply and sutures, including the strips of special ribbon-gut.

"How's it going, Ruthie?"

Ruthie Varden, an attractive, freckle-nosed, blue-eyed blonde, glanced at him and bulged her white mask with a quick smile.

"Fine, Dr. B., just fine. Be sure and give me warning when to start the twenty-minute saline-solution soak on the ribbon-gut. And look there on my reserve table and pin a medal on me—rib spreaders. Ruthie never forgets a surgeon's favorite idiosyncrasies."

"If you ever do, Ruthie, I'll perform a freckle-ectomy on your nose without anesthetic."

"Those X-ray plates get here?" he asked Hank, who nodded. "Put 'em in the viewer, please, and I'll be right with you." He stepped over to Joan Love, the circulating nurse, who was pouring medication into a stainless steel basin. "Joan, I guess you checked all the electrical equipment— lamp, suction, apparatus, defibrillator, et cetera."

"Of course, Dr. Beaumont."

"No offense." He went back to Ruthie. "Plenty of procaine on hand?"

"For instance, 150 mg. ready and waiting with syringe and long needle for intracardiac injection? Yes, Dr. Beaumont, I'm not up to a freckle-ectomy without anesthetic."

Hank had two X-ray plates, pyelograms, in the wall-slot viewers with the back lights on. The ladderlike spinal column was most prominent but the kidneys were visualized like ectoplasmic kites risen on the strings of the ureters leading up from the bladder. In one of the pyelograms both kidneys were on the left side of the spine. Matt pointed to it, saying to Shep and Hank:

"This could be mistaken for crossed renal ectopia. But this second pyelogram, where the right kidney is back over on its proper side, tells the story. A mobile kidney. Renal blood vessels and ureter serve as anchors but there's always a chance of its winding itself around the ureter and causing blockage, possibly subsequent renal dysfunction. As dangerous as that can become I'd usually chance it, but the adrenal gland is involved here. She's been having troubles that may very well be due to friction of the adrenal with

71

other vessels, nerves, muscles, caused by the kidney's wandering."

He switched off the viewer light. "We'd better scrub."

Walking to the other side of the operating room, Matt's glance touched the defibrillator, a boxlike instrument on wheeled legs. It featured voltmeter, ammeter, cords, switches, two cup-shaped, three-inch electrodes. Operating on 110 volts, 60 cycle A.C., variable resistance delivered $1\frac{1}{2}$ amperes. When the heart's muscles went into uncoordinated violent spasms and delivered no power, pumped no blood, a series of tenth-of-a-second shocks delivered by the defibrillator at one second intervals usually restored the regular beat.

Going down the short hall to the scrub room Hank said: "Dr. Beaumont, I thought you didn't believe in procaine for fibrillation."

"Except as a last resort, I don't. The defibrillator turns the trick, but just in case. . . ."

They stood side by side at the scrub room sinks, wet their arms via foot levers, lathered and brushed hands and nails thoroughly, and applied green, liquid, hexachlorophene soap and lather up to the elbows three times. Shep came in and started to scrub as they got sterile towels and dried their raised forearms carefully from fingertips down to the elbows.

They went into the operating room, got caps, masks, gowns from opened sterilized packs and dressed, with the circulating nurse tying the gowns in back. They worked on sterilized rubber gloves, wiped off the excess powder with moist gauze and went to the table.

Two orderlies and a floor nurse were wheeling Mrs. Metzger in. They transferred her with a lift sheet to the table; she had a uretal catheter and the orderly placed the drip jar on the floor. Semiconscious, her eyes uncomprehending and vaguely panicky, she moved her lips and half-smiled when Matt looked at her. Then her eyes closed as Bruce Fenton fit the face mask to her and intoned:

"Everything's all right now, Mrs. Metzger, just don't worry about a thing."

The orderlies and floor nurse remained and watched with the others, Ruthie keeping her gloves sterile and resting her hands in a muff on her gown. In four minutes Bruce Fenton said:

"You won't bother her. Go on and turn her."

Matt supervised her placement on her left side at the edge of the table. Braces were fitted into the kidney rest, front and back; he had the table broken, raised a few inches to a point just below her last rib, lifting her right side so the operational area was on a near straight line. Her upper leg was extended straight, the lower flexed. She was secured with straps across legs, hips and upper back.

Ruthie and Jane covered her with a sterilized laparotomy sheet, positioning the circular opening over the operational area, clipping the forward end to the ether screen. Bruce Fenton's assistant continued the anesthetic while Bruce began to attach the tubes for plasma and glucose infusions and continuous drip anectine, a muscle relaxant. Blood volume would be maintained and he'd be monitoring her venous and arterial pressure and pulse throughout the operation, alert to trouble.

Shep painted the exposed skin area. The main instrument stand, the suction machine tables with rinse basins, kick buckets for waste, the Mayo instrument stand, were all rolled in close.

"She's under." Dr. Fenton annouced.

"Check it," Matt ordered Hank. Ruthie swung the shelf of the Mayo stand out over the patient's hip.

"She's ready, Doctor," Hank reported.

Matt stepped up to the table, held one side of the incision line with a gauze compress between his gloves and the skin; Hank drew the skin taut with another gauze pad. His first cut went through skin, fat and fascia, to the muscle. Working easily, he began his usual query-and-answer routine with Hank and Shep about this case, its symptoms and possible consequences.

"Get the ribbon-gut soaking, Ruthie," he said presently.

Minutes later he remarked to Hank: "Now if we can find that wandering kidney."

His fingers probed into the opening, past towels, clamps, retractors and long handled hemostats.

"Ah, here we are. . . ." He brought the organ carefully up into the mouth of the wound. "Take it, Hank, gently; that's it; look at with your fingers. No tumors expected, none palpable. All right. Let me have it."

He opened the capsule, deftly stripped the organ out of its whitish bed of protective fat.

73

"The kidney itself is vital enough but this little area up here," he said, indicating the adrenal, "may unlock some of the mystery of life some day. Meanwhile, let's manipulate it as little as possible—Oh-oh. . . ."

He felt the quickened beat in the renal artery. He paused.

"How's the pulse, Bruce?"

"Steadied."

"Let's move on this thing!"

Using the ribbon-gut and attaching it through tiny slits, he made a form of sling for the total organ and fixed it to the twelfth rib, working in swift, silent concentration.

"There we are! Going home! Let's close up!"

The closure was without complications. He finished off with a figure 8 tension suture to hold the primary suture line and stepped back from the table. He took off his mask and went to the hamper, removing gown and gloves.

"Bruce, she's all yours."

Rescrubbed in Operating Room B thirty minutes later with the same crew, Matt was ready for his second operaion. He stepped up to the draped and prepared patient lying on his back on the table.

He began entry into the upper left quadrant of the abdomen with a paramedial incision down the the fascia, discarded the skin knife and cut the fascia with a clean knife. He and Hank clamped the bleeders, then ligated them with silk suture and discarded the clamps. After placing the skin towels and isolating the field, they paused to rinse their gloves in separate solution basins. Then, with Ruthie feeding them the required instruments and materials, they proceeded on down, retracting fascia and muscle layers, opening the tough sheath of the peritoneum.

The progress was rapid but unrushed, each position secured before continuing to the next step. Hank's speed and sureness of touch made the going smooth; they worked very well together, Matt noted for the hundredth time. He needed no more than his will to be capable of doing the whole procedure.

It was a Rankin aseptic method, anastomosis of the jejunum, which didn't require opening the intestine. In the peritoneal cavity itself Matt separated the diseased section of the small intestine from the mesentery and visualized it, bringing it up in a loop nearly two feet long. It was redly inflamed in some areas, pustulently yellow in others and there were extensive black patches of necrotic tissue.

"Not so pretty," Matt said as they put the section between clamps.

Bringing together the unaffected areas of healthy gut from above and below the diseased section, Matt began to apply continuous sutures before excising.

"This Fred Sarton's a lawyer and forty-five years old. He's a good case to think about when we get in discussions with our psychology friends. He's had gastric and duodenal ulcers for years, along with a lot of financial, professional and matrimonial trouble. Sure, the problems caused the ulcers, maybe even caused this thing we've got here—hand me the carbolicised knife and we'll psychoanalyze the thing the hell out and send it to Pathology—but this thing could kill, so what difference does it make now if it all began in kindergarten. And who's to say his adult problems, for the sake of his peace of mind, could or should have been avoided? Well, we're ready to close him up and get back to his troubles. Maybe in a few years we'll get some repeat business unless the psychologists improve their techniques."

They were removing sponges and laparotomy pads. The nurses were making the count before closure of the peritoneum when Bruce Fenton said from beyond the ether screen:

"Matt, you got any bleeding up there?"

"None," Matt said. He peered closely. "None."

"I'm losing volume. My systolic's dropping under sixty . . . fifty . . . forty .. ."

"Pulse?" Matt said. "I don't see any here . . ."

"Weak . . . slow . . . very slow . . . Matt, she's dropping like hell . . . twenty . . . ten . . . Nothing!"

"Nothing? No beat at all?"

"None. Full cardiac arrest."

There was sudden, total stillness in everybody in the operating room and a silence so complete that the nearly inaudible hum of the forced air through the wall and ceiling vents became loud.

The second hand on the wall clock was moving downward from 15 to 16 when Matt made his decision. He stripped off his right glove, caught up a knife from the instrument table and spoke sharply:

"Hank, cover that wound. Shep, unclip that side of the sheet from the ether screen."

He himself unclipped his side, swiftly exposing the chest.

"Epinephrin," Hank spoke to Ruthie, then called to Jane, "The defibrillator."

Matt shook his head, his hand on the exposed chest. "No! I didn't order them. Come here," he said to Hank.

Palpating the ribs he located the fourth intercostal space, placed his knife at the edge of the sternum and cut swiftly to the left.

"There's no fibrillation. But epinephrine along with the anesthetics would very likely cause it," he explained calmly. "This cut's between the fourth and fifth ribs. Don't bear down too hard, use a second cut to get through. Control it or you may rupture the pericardial sac."

The chest was open.

"Get your fingers in. Help hold the ribs open."

He inserted his hand. The heart was motionless, its tone flabby. He fixed the whole organ in his hand and began to squeeze and relax, squeeze and relax very swiftly. The second hand on the clock was at 29. When it touched 30, Matt began to pace his rhythm, two to the second . . .

Hank was staring at him, his deep-set dark eyes almost bugged and unblinking.

"I'm maintaining a one hundred-twenty per minute beat," Matt said. "I can't keep it up more than three-four minutes. If you're ever alone on this kind of thing don't try for more than eighty. But you and Shep can spell me off. Artery clamp, Ruthie . . . rib spreaders."

"Rib spreaders!" she ordered sharply.

"Shep," Matt said easily, "help him with the spreaders. Bruce, how're we reading?"

"Systolic up to sixty, rising. I'm on one hundred per cent oxygen. Should help."

"Cut it back down to about fifty."

"One hundred per cent is called for!"

"I'm in charge of this patient, Dr. Fenton," Matt said tonelessly. His voice dropped half an octave: "I'm not going to have him come out of the anesthetic with two open wounds and die from the pain shock. Cut back!"

"All right, all right. It's your responsibility if tissue anoxia kills him later. And if the brain goes without oxygen four or five minutes, you know what'll happen!"

"So long as he's got mind enough left to pay your fee and mine, it'll be all right. He was doing fine with twenty-one per cent oxygen till a minute or so ago. Fifty is plenty."

Hank and Shep had the rib spreaders on.

"That's good," Matt told them. "Hank, get in there and clamp the aorta below the arch. Increase carotid pressure up to the brain. Bruce is worried this fellow won't have wits enough to write a check for his fee."

Nobody cracked a smile. Hank was having trouble getting the clamp in the crowded space.

"Forget it . . . go in the abdomen, clamp the aorta there, as close up under the diaphragm as possible."

All the while Matt's right hand was squeezing a two-to-the second beat. He watched Hank trying to clamp the abdominal aorta. When he finished his forehead was glistening with sweat.

"Where's Jane . . . can't you see him sweat? Wipe him."

Jane came with sterile gauze, dried Hank, then approached Matt with a fresh cloth.

"Forget it," he motioned her away. "I'm dry . . . mop Shep, he's beaded . . . Ruthie, let's have 5 cc.'s of ten per cent calcium solution ready for injection in the left auricle. Shep, get your hand in here, take over from me . . . one hundred and twenty a minute . . ."

Shep stepped in, losing only a beat or two. Matt watched him for a few seconds. Ruthie was preparing an injection. Matt washed his hands, walked over and put on fresh sterile gloves.

"Should I unscrew this clamp a little, Doctor?" Hank called.

"No hurry. Get ready to spell off Shep."

Ruthie brought a syringe with the injection.

"Thanks. May use it, may not. In five more minutes I may want 0.3 cc. of 1:1000 adrenalin in 5 cc.'s saline. Hope not."

Twenty beats after he took over from Hank, Matt felt it —like a thrill coming up his arm to his shoulder and then washing over his whole body—the spontaneous beat from the heart. Matt held his hand motionlessly poised. He held his breath. He stared. He saw Hank, sweat running into his eyebrows, soaking his mask; he saw Shep, sweating, too. They were looking at his dry forehead.

"Pulse is only seventy!" Bruce Fenton bellowed. "You worn out, Matt? Get somebody else in there."

"Fred Sarton's in there!" Matt said. He laughed. He reached in with the syringe, injected the calcium chloride. He laughed again. "He'll wake up screaming that he didn't order any chest operation and damned if he'll pay. Now we've got two closures to make and we're behind schedule."

Finally the closures were made and the patient removed to the recovery room. Matt and Bruce Fenton accompanied him to alert the resident in charge about the special situation and the immediate postoperative problems.

On his return to the operating room Matt found Hank, Shep and the girls gathered at the linen hamper. Their talk stopped and they looked at him. He thought he saw respect on their faces. But an instant later he sensed that it was awe, as if they, and Hank in particular, were looking at a strange, fearful creature of another species.

"This isn't a social room. We need fresh packs, a new instrument setup for another laparotomy. Hank, I assume you're familiar with the case."

"You mean the next one, Doctor?"

"We're not rerunning Fred Sarton. I told Dr. Fenton to have Miss Ruedney here in twenty minutes. If you want any substitutes in the instrument setup, tell Ruthie before she phones the sterilized supply room."

Hank's dark, deep-set eyes seemed to bug slightly.

"Why would I want any changes?" he said nervously.

"It's a surgeon's prerogative," Matt said levelly, "to choose his own instruments."

"You don't mean *I'm* going to operate?"

Matt stared at him bleakly for a full ten seconds. Hank's gaze shifted, re-centered, shifted again. At last Matt spoke dryly:

"All right, then. Relax. I'll try to get George Cape or Jack Burton so if I have to go to the recovery room there'll be someone to take over."

Matt looked at Hank questioningly. A slow, dark flush began to spread over Hank's cheeks and there were glints of anger in his eyes.

"I'll do it!" Hank said grimly.

"Fine. Shep and I'll grab a smoke and coffee, then scrub. You be deciding if I'm first or second assistant."

Matt started away.

"So cool!" Hank said bitterly. "While I squirm! You don't care! About anybody!"

Matt turned back. "I don't like that, Dr. Simmons!"

"It slipped out. Nerves. Sorry."

Matt nodded and left the operating room, Shep with him. In the surgeon's dressing room Shep snickered.

"That was really throwing it at him, Dr. Beaumont. He'll make it. Hating your ice-cold guts every minute, but making it."

"He'd better," Matt said, lighting a smoke and inhaling deeply.

A half-hour later Matt stepped up to the table beside Hank. Ruthie handed them gauze compresses, put a skin knife in Hank's hand, her blue eyes expressionless. Hank cleared his throat, studying the exposed area.

"I will use a paramedial, rectus splitting opening, extending from here to here. Hold the skin, please, Doctor."

Matt pressed the gauze, pulling slightly against the compress Hank was holding on the other side of the proposed incision. The knife hovered, motionless. Hank's eyes, wide and dark above his white mask, cornered suddenly toward Matt. Matt could hear his open-mouth breathing. He lifted and withdrew the knife a few inches.

"Relax."

"Yes."

"She can't feel it."

"No."

"I'm right here. I won't let you go wrong. Make that incision!"

Hank extended the knife, lowered it. His gloved hand began to shake.

"Stand to the other side," Matt ordered, taking the knife from him. He proceeded with the operation. Relieved of responsibility, Hank assisted with his usual efficiency to the end.

"An easy one," Matt said, tossing his soiled gown into the hamper. "Shep, see if they've got Room A clean and set up for the next one. Girls, you better take ten. Hank, let's look in the recovery room."

Mrs. Metzger had already been sent to her own room. Fred Sarton, under blankets, was sleeping soundly, his general condition good.

Going down the hall to the dressing room, Matt said:

"That one really shook my confidence! Imagine my failing to suspect a heart problem. There's been one, definitely; that heart shouldn't have quit. I see what's been happening: his past ulcer problems masked and overlapped the heart symptoms. Well, let his own doctor worry about that."

"You didn't worry a bit when he might have died, did you, Dr. Beaumont?"

"You're asking if it was all the same to me if the patient lived or died," Matt said without rancor. "Idiotic question."

In the lounge Matt got coffee from the machine, sugared it heavily and watched Hank, his face sullen, draw a cup for himself.

"Fact is," Matt said without raising his voice, "it's your second insolence today. I could ground you. I won't because that's the easy way out you're looking for. Know what you're doing, Hank? Excusing your failure by accusing me. Seeing Beaumont as brute versus Simmons, the compassionate man, changes the good guy-bad guy picture. It's prettier for you that way."

Matt drained his coffee and went back to the urinals. He was washing his hands when Hank came in, his eyes downcast.

"I didn't mean to anger you, Dr. Beaumont."

"Anger's not the word," Matt said, drying his hands. He threw the wadded towel in the basket and walked back to his locker, got out a cigarette and lighted it. He sat on the bench trying to relax, but his neck was tense, the frown line between his brows deep. Seeing Hank at the end of the locker row he got to his feet, jabbed his cigarette toward him.

"Get over to A. The next one's yours, too. From initial cut to closure."

"Couldn't it wait? You saw what happened to me last time. I'm not up to it yet. I can't help it; I'm not as tough as you . . . I'm still shaking from that cardiac arrest."

"You weren't shaking after I took over on this last one."

"Well . . ."

"*Well* . . ." Matt mocked him. "In the name of humanity, Dr. Simmons, the good guy's gotta win! He can't just stand around feeling his noble sentiments and his crawling sweat while the bad guy's translating his skills into meaningful action in a crisis. This is a crisis, Dr. Simmons—Dr. Simmons' crisis. To be or not to be a surgeon."

"You're rough!"

"Rough!" Matt laughed harshly. "Surgery's rough. I did a lap once where I couldn't visualize the internal organs till we'd sucked out six quarts of free pus. We couldn't fully anesthetize a soldier in Korea with a crushed kidney and a liver full of steel splinters, and he moaned, screamed and wept almost every minute. One night in Chicago they brought in a gang-rape victim abused so viciously her anus was ripped out; we nerve-blocked the region and she was conscious. Every time I looked at her face she was crying heartbrokenly—a baby, twelve God damned years old. Rough? It can break you if you let it. Now, Hank, get over to A and get ready to use what you've got or you're no damned good!"

Hank lifted his trembling hands, looked at them then imploringly at Matt. "It's almost one o'clock. On top of everything I'm tired. It's unjust to judge me at my worst."

"Hank, surgery's not a game where things are fair or unfair. Emergencies won't always wait for a surgeon to be at his best. If his hands shake and his guts quake he's got a control problem. Solve it!"

Clearly he hadn't solved it when he took the knife for the skin incision. He began to stall and retreat, just as before. Matt changed tactics. He suddenly caught Hank's knife hand in his own free hand, his fingers grasping like steel. He felt the resisting tension in Hank's arm, saw the panic in his eyes.

"Relax your arm. That's an order!"

Hank was sweating and blinking. His whole body trembled. His arm locked against Matt. The tension seemed to grip everyone in the operating room. Matt maintained pressure, reinforcing it with a fixed, implacable stare into Hank's eyes. At last Hank's arm yielded. Matt bore down lightly and made the cut. Technically the incision was Hank's.

"Good," Matt said quietly.

The general feeling of relief surrounded but didn't include Hank himself. In the ensuing steps leading down to the actual surgical problem, he was slow. A nurse had to blot his forehead repeatedly. He had to get a fresh mask. Clearly he was fumbling worse every minute.

81

Watching hawkishly, Matt expended more nervous energy than he'd have used up in ten operations. Had Hank's wits been functioning he'd have known Matt wouldn't push him at the expense of the patient.

When the common duct was visualized Matt said easily, "Not bad, but it gets complex here and you're tensing up. Shep and I'll handle it. You walk around a little bit. But keep sterile so you can do the closure."

When Hank returned to the table he showed only a fraction of his real ability. Matt was forced to harangue constantly. ". . . you're not ready for that needle; those edges aren't approximated cleanly . . . that suture won't hold . . . clean that up before you go on. Look out, you're going to rupture that nerve sheath! Forget the clock; lost time's gone . . . don't rush . . . steady, there . . ."

When finally the patient was off the table, Matt went over to the hamper, ripping off his gown, mask, gloves, and swearing in a voice like cascading ice water.

Ignoring Hank, who was on the point of collapse, he said to Shep: "Minor operating Room L next. Phone and have the second patient started from her room twenty minutes after we start the first. We won't rescrub between them, so if we get good nurses, you and I can handle the two jobs in an hour and a quarter. If you need to grab a sandwich or something, O.K., but hustle it."

He started out of the room, still ignoring Hank.

"How about me?" Hank said.

"How about you?" Matt turned, shrugged. "Have lunch. A siesta. A stroll in the park. What difference about you?"

"Dr. Beaumont, you *know* I didn't want to fail."

"But you did."

"I'm not to have another chance?"

"Not at my patients."

"Just in one case my whole career is to be ruined?"

"Who ruined it?"

"You!" he shouted. "You, you bloodless, icy . . ." With effort he checked himelf.

Softened by Hank's truly desperate look, Matt spoke gently.

"I know you tried. And try to believe me, Hank, I don't want you to fail. If I've ruined you—and I don't think I have—I'd feel very badly about it. I've got blood enough for that. What I want you to do right now is write the

82

official reports on all four of these operations. Do you think you can have them ready for my countersignature by six o'clock?"

"No, sir."

"Make in nine, then."

"I can't by then, either—or ever!"

"They'll be done by nine tonight, Simmons! And mister, *they'd better be right!*"

Chapter Seven

Matt finished Monday's last operation at 3:14 and went to the surgeon's dressing room. Hank, using a dictating machine in the lounge didn't look up when Matt went through to the lockers to shower and change clothes. Awaiting him in his office on the second floor would be patients and a hill if not a mountain of messages, some important and some trifling, involving a score of past, current, future cases and entailing time-consuming phone calls, paper work, study of lab reports, records, case histories.

He wished he could by-pass the next few days' operations, consultations, examinations, complications and involvements of all kinds and step instantly into Friday afternoon. Judith Chalmers would be coming in then for her last visit before arranging to enter the hospital for the endocrine operations.

Leaving the surgeons' dressing room at 3:35, he was in a hurry. But word of the cardiac arrest case had spread through the hospital, and nurses, singly and in pairs and clusters, greeted him like a hero. He was stopped six times by a total of eleven colleagues. He'd have been a liar to deny he wanted and needed the approval of his world; but he was naggingly conscious of time. Still, it wasn't all lost; he took care of a few items, one with Arleigh Coleman, another with George Cape, that he'd have had to confer about later.

Mrs. Metcalfe, his office nurse, who'd retired as an R.N. and added secretarial work and bookkeeping to her considerable skills, wasted no time. While he went through the orderly array of folders and memos on his desk, she sent the afternoon's patients into the alcoves to undress; the first patient was already waiting on the examination room table.

"Miss Lassiter called. Do you want to call her back now?" Mrs. Metcalfe asked. When he shook his head she said: "Judith Chalmers phoned, confirming the appointment at three-thirty Friday."

"Good." He looked up, brightening. "How'd she sound?"

"She's not wavering, but of course she's surrounded by opposition. She's anxious to know the latest on the lab tests . . . me too . . . and she needs a booster shot of you."

"Get her, then, will you, Mrs. Metcalfe? I'll be dictating a summary of the tests tonight, but to summarize the summary for you: they came out great."

"I'm really glad, Doctor." She beamed and began to dial the phone. "Speaking of your magic touch, the chesty blonde was in again imagining that breast cancer you removed eighteen months ago is back. I offered to palpate for her." She laughed. "Seems only your hands will do. I threw her out . . . Hello, Dr. Beaumont calling Miss Chalmers, please . . . No, *Miss* Chalmers."

Matt took the phone and Judith came on.

"Hello, Dr. Beaumont?"

He smiled at the pretty lilt of her young voice, particularly nice because she often sounded as though she were using her last breath.

"How are you, Judith?"

"Imagine my doctor asking me that." She laughed. "Calm. Resolute. I should be resolute, shouldn't I, Dr. Beaumont?"

"You should. Absolutely."

"Ah-h-h. Good. I heard—well, I don't believe it, but I was worried—you might have to change your mind."

"Listen, dear. I finished those lab studies, and now I'm even more confident than before. I'm not changing my mind. Don't let anyone cause you worry or doubt about that."

"It was just that some doctor my father knows said the hospital might refuse you operating room facilities on my case. This doctor's a friend of Northside General's chief administrator."

"So am I, Judith. But even if this other doctor's opinion were to prevail, there are a dozen hospitals where we'll be more than welcome. Who was the doctor, d'you know?"

"No, I don't. I couldn't find out. But I'll try again if you want me to."

"I don't. I don't want you to aggravate yourself about

85

anything if you can help it. It doesn't matter who he is. You take care of yourself. See you Friday, Judith."

"I'll be there. Good-bye, Dr. Beaumont."

Merrijane Lacey, the last patient of the afternoon had just come up from the admitting office where arrangements had been made for her to enter the hospital in four days. In two weeks or so he would perform a heart operation. Merrijane was seventeen and looked thirty. Thin and wan, she had a hushed, whispery quality about her, and she moved slowly of necessity, hoarding her energies.

He knew her to be almost entirely undeveloped sexually, but there was a curious sensuality to her. The skin of her upper face, particularly around her eyes, was blue, as if grease paint had been applied for allure. Her lips were scarlet. Her coloring owed nothing to cosmetics, the blue and the scarlet alike were symptoms of her disease, mitral stenosis. There was a ghastly irony about her bright name and those bright lips below that almost literal, blue shadow of death.

She lived with her father and her aunt and, as on previous visits, they were with her. Physically robust themselves, an air of her enfeeblement clung to them as if they had slowed their own tempos in order to hold the closest possible contact with Merrijane.

It was clear in their every glance, touch and word to her that she was the center of their lives. It was a frail center that might last for years. Surgery could vitalize and extend those years, or reduce them to nothing. In nine cases out of ten he'd been successful with these operations. Merrijane Lacey looked to him like a "tenth." He had told them so. But such was the nature of these people's courageous love for the girl that they wanted him to go ahead. He hadn't wanted the case but he had become too sympathetically involved to turn back. When they'd left the office he realized suddenly how tired and emotionally drained he was, because he found himself yielding pointlessly to feelings of rage against Judith Chalmers' parents who wanted, against her will, to condemn her to perpetual half-life.

As he was phoning Vicky, she herself came into the office, sparkling with healthy color and sexiness. All smiles and warm kisses, she sat on his lap in his desk chair and put him back on the upswing. When he begged off from the hotel dinner he'd promised her, she took it in stride, sallying forth for food and bringing it back to share with him right there in the office. Then she made herself comfortable in the waiting room while he tried to catch up on work, including a close check on the generally acceptable operation reports Hank had sent down via Shep at seven o'clock.

At eight o'clock she was curled on the sofa, sleeping like a baby. He put a note in her prettily curled fingers saying he would be upstairs seeing patients for a few minutes. When he returned she was still asleep. He kissed her cheek to wake her. When she didn't stir he went back to his desk. She woke of her own accord in an hour.

She came padding in, shoeless and looking deliciously sleepy. She settled warmly on his lap, lay her head comfortably on his shoulder as if about to resume her slumbers. The feel of her refreshed his senses and rested his body.

"Hey," he said softly, "wake up. I'm lonesome."

"I'm awake, darlingest," she said. "I slept so nicely and felt so protected. I'm so proud I didn't get aggravated because you broke our date. I was mature, wasn't I, and understanding? And you were able to work better, weren't you, when you knew I was right here?"

"Yes, pet." He chuckled and nuzzled her cheek.

"It'll be that way when we're in our home. I'll know I'm safe and loved, and I won't have wild impulses. You'll know when you're working that I'm happy and loving you, won't you, darling? And I'd never let you down, and you'd never me." She dropped to a whisper, letting her lips tickle his ear. "Remember last night when we made our home ours?"

"It'll come to me in a minute." The memory and the immediate sensation of her body roused him.

"You want me powerfully, don't you, lover?" She squirmed subtly against him and giggled.

"Powerfully."

"We can use the examination table," she said excitedly, leaping up. She ran into the examination room.

"No," he cried in a kind of horror. He hurried, caught her and pulled her back, shaking his head. "Vicky, I've *told* you. I won't use that table for anything like that."

"It's sacred? I'd sully it?" she challenged, her green eyes flashing. "That's what my meaning is, compared with it?"

"Don't torture me, Vicky! I love you. You're the meaning outside of and above everything else. This, all of this, is pain-orientated, touched with death. Vicky, you're the other side, the life, the pleasure I need. Don't make me refuse you anything, sweetheart."

She studied him, her eyes narrowed, her mouth thrusting. After a while she seemed to decide something and relaxed.

"We'll go to my apartment," Vicky said contritely.

The next day the operational schedule was lighter. Hank, while below par, functioned reasonably well and Matt didn't pressure him. Wednesday he began to turn it on again, giving Hank hell on three different occasions, and instead of responding positively Hank seemed to deteriorate completely. By Thursday Hank had the air of a martyr. The chief surgical resident complained to Matt about him.

Fred Sarton, who'd have five or six critical hours Tuesday, was recuperating steadily.

Matt sent copies of the endocrine-studies summary to the consultants who originally opposed Judith's operation. He counted on a new consultation. Instead, they read the summary, met without him and reaffirmed their original stand. One by one he talked with them and, though personally friendly, their professional position was that he shouldn't undertake such a risky procedure. They wouldn't support him at a mortality conference or in court if he was sued for malpractice.

At 2:19 he was sure his colleagues' position of Judith's operation was final. At 2:20 he was doing something that made the hair crawl on the back of his neck. He was dialing Vicky, acting on mindless impulse, wanting to unload his disappointment on her, of all people.

By the time Vicky answered he had his wits back and didn't mention Judith Chalmers. They talked of other things and ended by assuring each other they couldn't wait till their date at nine, after she'd had dinner with her parents.

He was carried by her voice; when it was silent the disappointment settled again, like an actual weight on his chest and shoulders.

Three office patients with minor problems were disposed of; none of his hospital patients needed him. He'd looked forward to the free hours for some technical reading, some thinking, some planning, some speculation. Instead he sat staring emptily, fighting to keep his disappointment out of mind. It was impossible.

He went up to the Department of Pathology and into the big, bright, multicompartmented main lab. His pretext was flimsy, he thought wryly, but the reason was good. He wanted to look at somebody on his side, absolutely on his side, a loyal friend.

If this sympathetic spirit resided in the fine, clean-lined form of a soft-voiced, gently-eyed female, so much the better. He saw her from the windows of the central office cubicle where he was chatting with the assistant chief pathologist. She was on a high stool at a bench in an eight-girl line, her glossy dark hair gleaming above her white smock.

She was like some young priestess of modern magic, he thought proudly. Remarkably fine profile, he noted, almost classically feminine. He wanted to see Constanza full-face and feel the slow warmth of her recognition. She didn't turn. It would be unfair, if the girl imagined she was in love with him, to attract her attention. He went across to the hall door. Simultaneously she left her work. She followed him into the hall. He stopped and smiled at her.

"This is a lucky coincidence," he said

"It's not coincidence. I saw you when you came in." She gazed into his eyes. "It hurt me when you didn't come over and speak to me."

"I was chicken because I came specially to see you, Constanza."

"Honestly?" She bloomed, smiling. "Anything special?"

"No . . ." He was aware of their just standing, being pleased with each other and attracting glances from the numerous passers-by. "Let's walk along. I just needed my friend. You see, my associates think little of our endocrine studies. They're still telling me not to do the operation."

She stopped, leaned back against the wall, staring up into his face anxiously.

"That's terrible," she said huskily. "They're fools. They're contemptible. They've got no right to stand in your way!"

"They have their reasons, of course."

"Oh, sure they do," she said bitterly, her cheeks tingling with color. "All the smug, safe little people with their cozy little security always have reasons to oppose everything that's new and courageous and risky. Oh, I know they're successful men, and I also know the more successful they get, the more they're dedicated to their own comforts. They want to hold on to things as they are. They like the world small and orderly and anybody who ever tried to extend horizons has always been their enemy."

"Why Constanza, you feel very strongly about these things."

"Yes, and about you, because you're instinctively an outsider, like me. Contemptuous by nature of all compromise and of the trivial goals that 'nice,' righteous, safe, adjusted people live by. You live with your whole life. And you're going to make fools of them, Matt. They're not big enough, whoever they are, to tell you not to do that operation! You've made yourself *the* authority on it." She suddenly laughed at herself. "I'm afraid I didn't reach my conclusions by strictly scientific method."

"When a man comes to his friend, Constanza Vassily, for moral support," Matt said, looking at her wonderingly, "he goes not empty away."

"He goes not empty away," she assured him. "Well . . . I suppose I'd better get back. I wish— But, if wishes were horses, beggars would ride. Still, I wish . . ." she sighed.

"You wish me luck," he suggested.

"Exactly." She grinned at him and walked away, calling back, "Bye."

"Good-bye, Constanza."

Chapter Eight

The bandages were off Vera Dell's face. Matt made his way up to her room a little before seven with a rising sense of excitement and nervous anticipation. He joined George Cape who was pacing with an expectant-father expression on his strong, rough-cut face, and Arleigh Coleman, whose ulcer was evidently responding to the situation since his face was grim. He smiled with effort.

"Al Horner in with her?" Matt asked.

"Yes. Final make-up. She had her hair done, new dress—the works. We sent roses, so gimme three bucks." When Matt gave him the money, Arleigh added:

"Vera settled Dirken. Won't have him around. Good."

"Amen," George added.

At exactly seven Al, slimly handsome in a raw silk suit, opened the door and smiled.

"Well, fellow Pygmalions, Galatea awaits."

Matt went in last, shut the door and, drawing a long breath, joined the other men on the inspection line.

A tall, nicely proportioned, brown-haired stranger in a short, stylish little black dress stood by the bed, uneasy and unsmiling.

"Hello, Vera," George said. "You look lovely."

"Beautiful is the word, Vera."

"That's very nice of you, Dr. Coleman."

The newly molded face showed no trace of its former scars and distortions. It was a rounded oval and now that its lines were pleasing, the natural attractiveness of her unchanged lips was apparent. The work on her eyelids had done wonders for her hazel eyes. The others were enthusiastic, congratulating Al, and Vera. Matt saw, objectively, that it was a pretty face; he acknowledged it was a masterpiece of some sort.

"Hello, Vera." Matt said.

"Hello, Dr. Beaumont."

"Would you walk for us?"

"Surely. With my shoes on or off?"

"Both. A couple of times up and down the room."

She moved with ease, her hips fluid and free, and, turning, she remained in perfect balance and demonstrated that she could simultaneously bend to either side. Matt and the others watched and saw no evidence of the former limp.

"That'll be fine. No pain or anything?"

"No."

She stepped back into her new black pumps. On the bed was a long-handled vanity mirror and four roses she'd snipped from the vaseful on the table. She took one rose and going to Al she put it in his buttonhole.

"Dr. Horner, I want to thank you for everything you've done for me." She rose on tiptoe and kissed him. "Anything I can ever do to repay you I will. Anything."

She presented the rose, the kiss and the identical speech to each of them in the same toneless voice. It was dutiful, lifeless, embarrassing.

"That was very sweet," George said fatuously, "and so are you. Don't let us stop you from looking at that lovely face in your mirror. We know you're dying to."

"Go on, honey," Al urged, beaming like a schoolboy.

"Don't mind us," Arleigh said, grinning.

"Well . . ." Vera said. Only she and Matt failed to catch the party spirit.

"She doesn't want to," Matt said.

Vera looked at him steadily for several moments. "You're the only one who didn't say you liked my face. Why?"

"Do you?"

"Very much!" Hastily she caught up the mirror, glanced in it and away. "But naturally it's strange. I don't know myself yet." She peered at herself more closely, as if she were back at her lab job bringing something into focus under a microscope, something like a cancer-suspect tissue specimen. "But I just love the new me." She smiled glassily.

The men looked uncomfortably at one another. Matt shook his head.

"You don't mean it, Vera."

George Cape stared at her, his head cocked at that listening angle. "I have daughters, dear, and occasionally when I buy them something they're disappointed, and this makes me unhappy. You're afraid of making me unhappy now, so you should know that I never become unhappy about criticisms directed at Dr. Horner."

Vera laughed for the first time; Matt and the others joined in.

"You're our girl. We've got a big emotional stake in you, Vera," Al Horner said. "We understand you've been anxious that your face might not be a success. Physically it is a success. Emotionally you're still afraid of it. You're an intelligent girl and you've had time to think about your life from here on out, but the problem obviously isn't solved yet. As you know, Miss Tanner's going to be helping you with your psychological re-adjustments. Your friends and family will help you. Dr. Cape, Dr. Beaumont, Dr. Coleman and I are at your disposal if you get in trouble or need money or advice.

"We'd have staked you for a few months, helped you get another job. Since you want the old one back, it's yours, and everyone in NSG is happy you'll be on your way again next week. At first you may have trouble concentrating on work, but everyone will understand, Vera. You'll have to hold tight. Men will want to make love to you and what scares you is you'll want them to. At the same time you dread promiscuity . . . Ah, look, look at that color in her face!" he exclaimed. He touched various spots on her face. "See? The blood supply's well established."

Vera giggled nervously. "Blood supply-wise, I'm great. Too great, maybe. All over my body."

"You mean genitally, of course," Arleigh Coleman said. "Well, you're no longer in a frenzy to grab just anything in pants. Remember, a pretty girl can pick and choose, with time and mind on her side. If," he amended after a pause, "she wants it that way."

"You can imagine what I want." She sat on the bed, crossed her ankles and tugged her skirt over her knees. "I'm scared of disgracing all of you. I'm not at all determined to resist temptation." She spoke looking down at her lap, then looked up anxiously from one to another. Her gaze lingered on Matt. "There's something else. I think you sensed it, Dr. Beaumont. Something . . . oh, dark. My feelings about being ugly and about beauty. I don't know how to express it—not without alienating the four people in this world that I love, you four."

"Go on." Matt told her.

"I adjusted to being ugly by turning to other matters, to learning and working, to building character and pride. I told myself these were better things. If I had feelings of love to express and I wasn't allowed to because I was ugly, I understood and accepted. Every time a man was repelled by me but instantly charmed by a pretty face, no matter how empty it might be, I accepted the facts I was forced to accept. But I came to hate every pretty face. Hate them murderously. I still do. And here I am wearing one of their faces!"

She got up and went to the window, came back slowly. "I don't want to hate anything. I want to seduce. I want to be seduced. I want to be told love-lies and tell love-lies and give myself to everybody, even the four of you, *especially* the four of you—to four hundred, four thousand. I'm crazy and craving and insatiable . . ." She poured it out, and the more she talked the more animated and genuinely pretty she became.

Fortunately she had numerous other visitors due and they made way for them. They walked down the hall in a subdued mood. George was particularly glum.

"Imagine. Four thousand lovers!"

Matt laughed. "Don't worry, George, she'll settle for half that many. And we won't let her rape you."

"Really, you're damned flippant about it. What've we done to the girl?"

Matt looked at him scornfully. "Al gave that girl a face that is like opening a prison door for her. So what's been 'done to the girl' has given her freedom. Is she entitled to it only if she uses it according to your rules of virtue, or mine, or Al's or Arly's? Let's not climb on a pulpit; let's have a little more confidence in her."

"To hear a tyrant lecture on freedom is among the lesser amusements."

"Who the hell's a tyrant, George?" Matt asked. He and the others stopped in the semiprivate area of a corridor turn.

"One who uses his strength against the weaker—you."

"That's a very serious charge, George." Matt stared at his solemnly accusing face. "I don't understand you."

"This doesn't concern Vera," Al Horner said. "And I've got to catch a plane so I'll say good-bye."

94

There was a pause for amenities as Al left. Then Matt looked at George Cape. Their professional bond of high mutual regard was the one Matt considered strongest in the whole hospital. Now George's expression was disturbingly hostile.

"You were entrusted with developing one of the best young surgical prospects I've seen in years, a talented fellow bringing sensitivity along with brains into the profession. Directly after a cardiac arrest, a dreadful emotional experience for any feeling person, you forced him to perform beyond his present ability. And again and again you've bludgeoned him emotionally until now Hank Simmons has been driven beyond the break point."

"Beyond the break point!" Matt said. "First I heard of it. What'd he do? What happened?"

"He broke. He's sick in bed. Since mid-afternoon. Initial tests on the physical level show nothing, chiefly because it's his spirit you've sickened. He was on the ward and saw that cardiac-arrest patient, Fred Sarton, then the young girl, Dorothy Ruedney, whose operation followed Sarton's and was the one Simmons first failed on. Just after this, he went on sick call, looking like a ghost. The connection is obvious."

"He wasn't pushed beyond his capacity. He's capable of almost every procedure in the book," Matt said tightly. "He's afraid of the responsibility. What I've actually done is handle him too gently. I should have forced this issue months ago. But this is no place to talk about this."

The three men went to the empty lounge of the surgeon's dressing room. Matt paced and smoked while George Cape renewed the attack and Arleigh Coleman listened.

"The nurses, the floor and operating room supervisors, Bruce Fenton and assistant, orderlies, everybody, confirm Hank Simmons' story, that you handled that cardiac-arrest dreadfulness as if you were excising a mole—coldly, with scarcely a drop of sweat, when everybody else had their shoes full."

"I saved a man's life. I'm not going to apologize for noncomformist sweat glands, or failure to panic along with the women and boys. Nor do I propose to defend my judgment in the proper handling of Hank to you, George—or to you, Arly. And I resent the implication I'm lacking in human feeling. I consider your interference damned presumptuous."

95

"Sensitive on this, aren't you," Arly said. "You know what's on the grapevine? An episode in young Dr. Beaumont's career. The judgment of no less than Dr. Adatti himself, that Intern Beaumont was unfit to be a surgeon because he was an ice-cold heartless bastard. History repeats itself."

Matt paled. His voice quivered. "Who dug up that old dirt?"

"A man I despise: Dirken," George said. "He's been after you. A man's life spreads, branches; there are a hundred places he could have made contacts with people who knew you then. He did get a story. Is it true?"

"Yes. But from what you've known about me for years, George, and you, Arly, would you have judged me a machine? Except for this old thing and the rotten business of that cardiac arrest?" He stared, demanding an answer.

"Well," George said, "on the basis of my own experience with you, your attitudes, your successes, your . . . well, no, except for this, Matt, I would not so judge you."

"Arly?"

"Same. But the well is poisoned, Matt. George and I aren't spreading rumors, but they're spreading nonetheless. We try stopping them . . . but Matt, if you go ahead on this damn fool endocrine gland operation—"

"Arly, if it was a damn fool thing, would five or seven endocrine specialists have confirmed me with formal opinions the operation is theoretically possible?"

"Theoretically!"

"I'll take it out of the realm of theory!"

"You'll be gambling. Lose, and you lose one patient and your mortality rate is good enough to sustain it. Win, and maybe you're famous and the Beaumont method will go into the books. That's what enemies will make of your motives. I don't think you think that way, but—"

"But suddenly you don't know. Well, let it remain a mystery. Watch the show. When you know how it comes out it'll be safe to choose up sides. Good night."

He turned and walked to the exit door.

"Don't go off in that spirit," George called after him.

He didn't answer.

He saw two pre-operative patients, looked in on his recovering postoperative patients. Mrs. Metzger was up and scheduled to leave Saturday; the same with Miss Ruedney and old Mr. Davis; all of them hoping in the pleasantest possible way that he, or the painful necessity he represented, was out of their lives for good. Fred Sarton, who'd innocently cast him in the double role of hero-villain, was sitting up in bed, talking and laughing; he at least was sure Matt Beaumont was: "Man, the greatest!"

Here and there the averted face of a nurse or a doctor reflected a change in mood toward him. He sensed it or imagined it, he didn't know which. He shrugged and made his way to the intern's quarters and rapped on Hank's door.

"Come in. Oh, Dr. Beaumont. Thanks for coming."

It was a small, dismal room, equipped with two cots, table and straight chairs, bureau and lockers. Hank was alone in one of the cots wearing a dressing gown; a textbook, a magazine and an ash tray were on one of the straight chairs between the cots. Hank started to clear the chair. His face was drawn.

"Don't bother, Hank. I'll park on the other cot. I just found out you went on sick call. How are you feeling now?" Matt asked.

"Rotten."

"How come?"

Hank turned his face to the wall. He looked utterly miserable.

"Cigarette?" Matt said, taking out a pack.

"Huh-uh . . . thanks."

Matt lighted one for himself. Hank turned his head and stared at the ceiling. Matt leaned back against the wall, smoking in silence. Hank neither looked at him nor spoke. Nearing the end of his cigarette, Matt sat forward.

"Well, Hank, this is pointless. We don't get through to each other any more. If you want a transfer to another surgeon . . ."

Hank turned sharply, his eyes panicky. "You're dumping me?"

"No. But I'd sign a transfer, if you want that. Maybe you can't benefit from further association with me. It's harder to learn from someone you're hostile to."

"It's not you but me I hate. You showed me myself—raw. I'm not up to the demands. I'm not the man you are. You've always been correct in your personal estimate of me."

97

"Are you crazy? My personal estimate! Why, I was on the intern committee that selected you in the first place. Then I grabbed you for personal training—a doctor I deemed worthy of this profession; someone I was anxious to teach the best of everything I knew."

"And you did. Conscientiously, for three years. Despite a personal aversion, you believed I was good for the profession and you owed it to the profession. But I'm not up to it, and now you know it. I will never have the kind of cold will and strength you have. I won't be a lesser surgeon than you are; I'll be as good or better—or nothing—and that's what I am: nothing!"

"I won't cater to this self-pity. I won't sit here and listen to that infantile pap coming out of a man's mouth. Get up off your ass, and quit feeling sorry for yourself. You'll be at work in the operating room tomorrow morning on schedule."

"You can't be that callous, Dr. Beaumont. You can't be."

"I am."

Hank sat up, shaking his head violently. "No. You're not. You're doing what you conscientiously think is best for me. You're being my guts, forcing me to be a man. It hasn't worked, but you're committed to seeing it does work. You want to do right. You think you are doing right," he said with rising agitation. "I'm sorry. You don't understand. A man with broken legs *can't* walk. I would if I could . . . but don't you see, don't you *see*?"

Suddenly tears were running down his cheeks. The sight of it twisted something in Matt. A man, a good man, sitting there broken, crying like a kid; it tore at him agonizingly. He wanted to turn away, to shield Hank from being seen in this state. Instead he stepped across, put an arm across his back and gripped his shoulder.

"You mustn't break, kid. You just mustn't. I'm sorry if I've done this to you, Hank. Forgive me. I'm for you, not against you. My God, don't you know that? How I feel about you and Shep? What it's meant to me to see you learning and growing professionally? You and Shep are my first interns; if you were my flesh, my first-born son, I couldn't be more involved with your future. Can you think I want to ruin you? Can you think my strength is against you? It's *for* you, for God's sake. You'll break my heart if you fail, you damned fool!"

He left the room, giving Hank a minute or two to compose himself. Then he re-entered. He extended his hand, waited till Hank took it. Matt shook his hand, clasped it in both of his for a moment. Stepping away he said:

"We're different types, Hank, with different reactions, not different species. I'll see you in the scrub room tomorrow. Good night!"

When Matt arrived at Vicky's apartment, she was waiting eagerly and rushed into his arms. He held her close and kissed her softly rather than feverishly.

"You're tired," she said, and helped him settle in his favorite place, a long, shallow crescent of sectional furniture with his feet out on a hassock. "I've got drinks," she said.

She hustled to the kitchen and reappeared with a shaker of vodka martinis and glasses on a tray. She was in lavender satin pajamas with voluminous legs that swished and flapped as she walked; her hair was drawn back, dripping at her nape like a loose double handful of flame.

As she stood bent forward over a low table pouring the drinks, he enjoyed her profile. She saw him admiring her and smiled happily.

She stationed herself beside him, her legs doubled under her, and sat facing him, her knees and thighs together. She turned gracefully to the table and handed him his drink. Then taking her own she sipped and smiled at him. With her hair away from her face her dazzling green eyes seemed larger, more compelling than ever. She laced one hand with his and rested it on the lavender satin slope of her thighs. When he drained his glass, she drained hers and refilled them both.

She set her drink down, got up and went over and put on a record. It was instrumental music, soothing, slow, sweet. Returning, she drifted and glided and circled in an impromptu dance. She was so pretty, so graceful, so pleasing to the eye and the heart, he thought, watching her with a kind of sadness. She came back, and placed ash trays and lit cigarettes for them both and sat close against his side, drawing his arm around her body. He held her tightly, his hand inert on the soft, luscious rounding of her warm hip.

"What's wrong, Matt?"

"Whatever there is. You name it, it's wrong."

99

"Do you want to talk about it?"

"Vicky . . . I don't know where to begin."

"Just any place, darling."

"You remember I mentioned I almost lost a patient Monday, a heart-stop? Well . . ." He traced in for her the situation in general, including George Cape's criticisms and the talk about him at NSG. He spoke to her for the first time of his crucial experience as an intern; he touched on Hank; Vera Dell. The cocktail shaker was empty when he finished.

"Anybody who knows you, knows you're not callous. I know it. Honey, did the drinks and talk and me ease you off? Would you like to be loved?"

"I'm so relaxed I'd like to use that bed for something pretty wild—sleep. Give me a half-hour."

"I'll take you in and get you comfortable, then remove all temptation."

He loosened his clothes, took off his shoes and stretched out exhaustedly, his face down on the bed. She knelt on the floor beside the bed till her face was level with his on the pillow and gazed smilingly into his eyes, and stroked his face.

"Sleep well, sweetheart."

He reached out and caressed her, then he shut his eyes and was instantly asleep. The lavender of Vicky's pajamas was the last thing he saw. He seemed to have closed the color in under his eyelids, for it formed the twilight atmosphere in which he was floating slowly downward. The lavender deepened to purple to black to thick pitch—black. His feet touched wet, cold stone. He was in an immense central chamber of a prehistoric stone cave. Somehow he knew that eight passages, like octopus arms led out from this central chamber.

He stood blind in the darkness, unmoving, but there was an invisible motion toward the edge of total silence. He was suddenly shatteringly past silence. Thunderous roaring, powerful engines were speeding through the octopus arms toward the center. They came racing, the volume of their sound deafening. He couldn't see them. He couldn't move forward or back or anywhere except within himself, and he had to reverse his life and ungrow, shrinking rapidly to a third his size.

One of the speeding automobiles crashed and a girl with a beautiful face, suddenly illuminated, came hurtling through the windshield directly at him. It was the face of Vera Dell in the instant before it was first scarred. Her mouth was open in a silent scream . . .

There was another shuddering crash from a greater distance. Two young women together came hurtling at him: his Aunt Sally-Dee and his mother in the instant before their deaths, and his heart stopped and he took a knife and opened his own chest and reached his hand in and pumped his heart.

Merrijane Lacey's scarlet-lipped, mitral-stenosis face, then Judith Chalmer's face joined the gallery and they hung waiting while he pumped his own heart. His arm began to grow tired and he started to cry. His body was covered with sweat and there was no one to relieve him, and his strength was failing, weakening, draining out of him . . .

He woke on his back on the floor, one clenched fist on his chest. His heart pounded. The nightmare's cold terror clung to him. He tensed when the door opened from the lighted front room. Vicky peered in.

"Matt!" she cried. "What's wrong?" She dropped beside him, looked closely into his face.

"A dream," he said hoarsely. "It's all right . . . now that you're here." He lifted himself on his elbows. In shock he stared down his body. He appeared to be sexually fervent, though he was passionless. It was as if that death dream had called out a profound instinctive assertion of the life force. Vicky looked, too, and stood up slowly.

"I'll say you had a dream!"

She stood above him, gazing down expressionlessly while she fingered the hip of her pajamas. The pants dropped with a whispery sound, brushing his shoulder and exposing her slim, beautiful legs. When he sat up she deliberately stepped across him, her thigh touching his face, then with a turning swing of her naked hips she sat on the bed.

He grinned at her and pulled off his undershirt while she sat unbuttoning her pajama coat, her arched, pretty feet moving sensually on his lap. He kissed her knees and stood up. She gazed up, her eyes smoky, her underlip looking poutily swollen. The pajama coat dropped from her shoulders, and she thrust out her bare, soft, pink-nippled breasts proudly, then lay on her back, one knee lifted, the other leg extended full length.

The feel and the scent of her silky, perfumed flesh and

the sweet taste of her mouth as he positioned her delicious body under his dissolved every trace of that death dream. The throb of his thrusting passion was the pulse of life and he entered the embracing, healing heat of her body joyously.

And when they were done, finishing with a burst of ecstasy, he could not, he would not withdraw. He held her there, her legs locked around him, and clenched her buttocks in his hands and remained a part of her, bound to her.

"I love you . . . you're my life!"

He kissed her mouth, and her lips clung to his and her tongue danced fierily against his. After a few minutes his whole male force was at peak again and he began to move in a jolting violent rhythm that made her cry out in sharp excitement.

Afterwards they both slept, exhausted. It was five in the morning when he woke, fresh and strong. She lay, warmly naked, beside him. He kissed and stroked her and she woke and stared at him. Her eyes began to flood with tears.

"What . . .?" he cried, bewildered.

"It was so total, so complete the way you loved me, the way I loved you. To think of losing that, Matt. To think of anything ever separating us, destroying the chance of our home, our children, our futures, our happiness. I can't stand it!"

"Darling, nothing can come between us."

"Oh, yes. Yes. I know one thing you didn't tell me about when you were talking about your troubles: that girl, Judith Chalmers. You held that in. You couldn't give that to me. Oh Matt, don't you see what can happen if you fail? If you're antagonizing other doctors already, if your reputation is hurt, if confidence in you is shaken, patients won't be referred to you. Your income, even if Mr. Chalmers didn't sue for malpractice, which he will, will be cut off or go down so far there'd be no hope of finishing paying for our home or maintaining it.

"I'd have to go with my head down to my father and tell him what he'd like to hear, that you can't take care of me, that he'll have to save us. Oh, Matt, it needn't be. You needn't jeopardize anything. This thing is too big, too much is at stake. It's a shard inside you; get it out, Matt. Take away that conflict, that pain. You're not required to play God. You do all you can for everybody it's possible to do for. But, Matt, Matt, please don't do this to *us*. Don't take that chance. Don't gamble with *my* life."

"Vicky, I need you. I need you with me. You're my strength, my heart. Don't stand against me. All I've got to justify my whole damned existence is my work; don't make me dishonor it, Vicky. Please. God, don't ask this of me, Vicky."

"You can't be dishonoring your profession when your own colleagues say it's not only unrequired of you but *wrong* of you!"

"I *could* use that as an excuse, Vicky, to squirm out of my own decision. Except I *know* I can do it. I *know* they're wrong. Of course there's a risk, but not enough to justify my quitting, and breaking my promise to a patient and breaking my own . . . well, sense of honor."

"Matt!" She was suddenly sharp, her eyes hard, her mouth setting tightly for a moment. "You listen to me! It's vital to me that you abandon that operation. I insist on my right to ask this of you. You want me, Matt, you need me. You need me more than you know. That nightmare of yours last night, the compulsiveness of the way you loved me, shows you're not so invulnerable!"

"No, I'm not," he said dully. "But—"

"Then you're going to hold on to what you have to have emotionally, Matt. Patients give you nothing. They come and go and hope they never get in a spot where they have to see you again. You're starved for love, for continuity, for a home, for me. I'm what you need and want."

"Yes, more than anything."

"You'll call it off, then—Judith Chalmers' operation?"

He looked down and sighed. He shrugged. He lifted a palm, let his hand drop.

"Yes."

"You mean that?"

"I said it, Vicky."

She hugged and kissed him, laughing jubilantly. "You're my man, Matt, you're my man. Come on, lover, we'll shower and I'll fix breakfast and we'll go see our house by dawn light. You'll see, you'll never regret this!"

103

Chapter Nine

Hank appeared dramatically, looking like a sleepwalker, in the midst of the busy preparations for the first patient in Operating Room A.

"Better late than never," Matt said. "The patient's on his way. Let's scrub. You can make it?"

"I can make it," he said sullenly.

"Only two this morning," Matt said to him and Shep when they were at the scrub room sinks. "The first's a victim of a quack who treated him for hemorrhoids for years. Meanwhile, his cirrhosis has advanced till we'll have to cut out half his liver and hope he'll have enough left to last him the rest of his life.

"You'll have a chance with that liver tissue to improve your mattress sutures, Hank. Nothing special about the other one: the compound leg fracture. Except, always be alert in these traumatic fractures to the problem of clots and the release of fats into the bloodstream which can lead to pulmonary embolism and . . ." he clapped his wet hands loudly . . . "sudden death. So never go into these cases as if they're just bone-setting."

They were done by eleven o'clock.

"Well, young doctors, I understand you've got thirty-six hours off starting at noon. You're free now, as far as I'm concerned. I'll write the operation reports myself. You can get your programs of dissipation and lechery underway any time. Rarin' to go, Hank?"

"No, sir, Dr. Beaumont," he said, as if answering a formal question, his manner resentful, barely civil, as it had been all morning. "May I ask your opinion of my work today?"

"Poor, Hank."

Hank smiled faintly, like a just man enduring injustice. "I'm sorry, sir."

"No, unfortunately, you're glad. It proves to you that I was wrong in ordering you to work. It's a kind of win for you; but don't be too sure you've scored even that much. Maybe your work wasn't poor. My aggravation with you may be prejudicing me. In case that's so, I'll refrain from entering a critical notation on your progress record. Now, if you'll excuse me."

Judith Chalmers was his only appointment that afternoon. He had plenty of work to keep him busy: two consultations, visits to Pathology, Radiology, Fluroscopy, phone calls, reports to read. But as the zero hour of 3:30 approached, his concentrative capacity dwindled. He couldn't decide *how* he'd tell her, whether to be crisp, decisive, efficient . . . impossible! He'd assume the manner of a stuffed owl, wise, pompous old Dr. Beaumont, bumbling with words such as reconsideration, reconsultation, necessity for judgment revision . . . He was sick at his stomach.

At 3:10 he heard voices, including Judith's, out in the waiting room.

Mrs. Metcalfe came in. "The whole tribe is here," she told him. "Her father and mother and her fiancé. And, Dr. Beaumont, I regret telling you, the parents brought Dr. Amos Dirken. He's asked to sit in."

"I'll extend that courtesy."

"You will?" She looked at him anxiously.

"Thank you," he said, in a tone of dismissal and began arranging the chairs, bringing in two extra straight-backed chairs from one of the examination rooms.

Judith came in first, a fragile, almost wispy girl with very fine, pale-blond hair. Her color was high with excitement, her blue-grey eyes shone. More often the skin was pasty, the eyes lusterless as slate.

She would pay for this hour of exaltation with a day, two days, perhaps, of exhaustion. Her peaks of vitality rose quite high, and from such vistas she dared to dream, to hope, to love. But the plunges were deep and prolonged and, though she would see the heights from her depths, she was physically incapable of reaching them. To sustain normal sexual intensities was within her power, but a serious drain on her energies. To bear the children she craved would be totally beyond her in her present condition.

She wore, as did her mother behind her, an open mink coat. Under it was a pale-blue spring-tone suit, a white blouse, a sparkling brooch, probably diamond. She put her hand in Matt's and smiled winsomely.

"I'm glad to see you, Dr. Beaumont. Do I sit there at your right hand?"

"You do, Judith . . . it's the 'pretty girl' seat. I thought you'd like this fellow beside you."

"Oh, yes," she said, giving her fiancé a look verging on worship. "You've met Van, haven't you, Doctor?"

"Of course. Good to see you again, Van."

"I'm right here with her and you, Doctor, not with them. We told them to get off your back, but we couldn't stop 'em coming."

"It's quite all right, quite all right . . ."

Matt nodded at Mrs. Chalmers and her husband who seated themselves in front of his desk, and at Dirken, who stayed on his feet.

Durken, his round pink face and Santa Claus figure exuding fraudulent good will, smiled benignly on everyone and unleashed a profusion of pieties about his confidence in the noblest intentions of all concerned, and began thanking Matt for allowing him to sit in on his case. Matt cut him off.

"You're welcome. Have a seat," Matt said, settling in his own chair. He opened a box of cigarettes, gestured it toward the parents who ignored it, toward Van and Judith who declined. He lit one for himself.

He gazed thoughtfully at Mr. Chalmers, a heavy-set, moonfaced man with a petulantly down-curving mouth and slaty eyes, whose expression of hostility was the only one Matt had ever seen.

"I came hoping you could get me in the hospital right now, today," Judith said anxiously.

"There's no bed space just now, Judith."

"When do you think?"

"Well . . ." Matt swung his swivel chair around to face the window. He got nervously to his feet. "It might be a month. This isn't an emergency, you see, and . . ." He frowned deeply, turned his chair and sat at his desk. "It would probably be best all around if—"

"Dr. Beaumont," Judith cried. "What're you thinking? Tell me, tell me. I don't understand your attitude, your evasiveness . . ."

Mr. Chalmers cleared his throat. "Judith, my dear, he's trying to confess the truth, finally, that the operation on

106

which you built your pitiful hopes, my poor darling, would have been a cruel hoax, useless at best, deadly at worst."

"Shut up, Mr. Chalmers," Matt said softly, looking only at Judith, who was staring at him almost in shock. "Judith, are you sure you want this operation? Do you *know* that you *must* have it?"

Her mouth had become colorless; her skin was blotchy; her lips trembled and she began to hold her throat, massaging it. "I believe in it. If you don't . . ." Her voice faded. "If you don't any more, I'll . . ." She couldn't go on. She put her fingers to her mouth, gnawing at them, and just stared, her eyes terrible, for they were the eyes of the abandoned, the defenseless, and even as he looked their luster dulled, the blue somehow fading. She slumped in the chair, torpid.

"Van," Matt said quietly. "Take her back to a cot. I'll ring for the nurse to help you. And you tell your girl, you tell her that . . . that I'm sorry to have frightened her this way. But now we know her whole will to live is authentically with us. She's going to fight all the way. And so am I. I believe in that operation—as much as ever. And," he swiveled, his glance raking her father and mother and Dirken. "Nobody's going to stop me!"

"I've warned you, Beaumont," Chalmers shouted.

Van was trying to move Judith.

"No," she protested. "No. I don't want to lie down. Let me stay. Dr. Beaumont, I inherited money from my grandparents. I'll have my will rewritten to pay the full amount of any malpractice suit judgment against you."

Her father got to his feet and bellowed at her: "You've let that fortune hunter and this quack turn you against me."

"Stop this, please," Matt raised his voice authoritatively. "I'm not going into anybody's will. No one will have occasion to sue. I'm not trying to take your daughter from you—"

"She's a sheltered girl. Always was weak and sheltered," Chalmers cut in. "The emotional rigors of marriage, even to the right man—"

"Nobody would ever suit *you*." Judith cried.

"—would crush my baby. I love her. I won't let that happen, you quack!"

"She's not your baby, Mr. Chalmers, but a woman. She'll be capable of living as one. Would you deny her that natural right, a right her worst enemy would concede her?"

"You have a vile mind, Dr. Beaumont."

Dirksen said: "Now Mr. Chalmers, consider the source. We've got to stay with the central issue. It's not marriage versus innocence, but life versus death, with Dr. Beaumont in favor of death. No, no, Beaumont, your laugh is not going to reduce this to absurdity, nor turn me into a fool. Your colleagues told you in formal consultations, before and after your mouse studies, that your operation would *kill that little girl* !"

"Dirken," Matt warned, "these fright tactics are disturbing my patient."

"I am not going to be scared off!" Judith said.

Van glared at Dirken, then looked uncertainly at Matt. "Did they? Your colleagues?"

"No. They point out dangers of hyperirritation of the heart, resultant from manipulation of the glands in question and the nerve system. This I've anticipated. As I pointed out to them, I'm fully prepared to meet and prevent any such complications."

"Beaumont's an authority on heart-stop during operations in a case he forgets to anticipate. Just last Monday, in fact, a man died on the table. But Dr. Beaumont cut open his chest dramatically and hand-pumped the fellow's heart. And damned if he's not alive and kicking right now."

"Restrain yourself, Dirken, or I'll have to ask you to leave."

"But I'm *crediting* you—"

"By bringing up a terrifying specter of possible death under my hands. Leave this girl alone!"

"Forgive me, Judith. But you should know *how* Dr. Beaumont will handle emergencies with you."

"Not handle emergencies—anticipate and prevent them!"

"Of course. But to continue—other surgeons feel, and many of these men have better reputations than Dr. Beaumont, and much more experience, they feel that even assuming that he will be able to walk across a mined field, avoiding all the explosive possibilities and the procedure is a success, the benefits are more a matter of his wishful thinking than proven scientific fact.

"Oh, he has told us about the theoretical confirmation he has from endocrinologists. He claims he proved something with mice and guinea pigs. Nonetheless, at best, the girl will have a cruel letdown. She'll be unimproved, probably harmed, if she lives. She must face the fact her condition is incurable at the present stage of medical knowledge."

"Get out of my office, Dirken. And the rest of you, too. Except my patient and, if she wishes him to stay, her fiancé. Not another word, Dirken!"

"I'll sue you. I'll sue you penniless, damn you," Chalmers said as he left. "If it's the last thing I do!"

His wife was incensed. "He *is* a machine. Dr. Dirken warned us he was. What difference does it make to him if a man's heart stops or somebody's little girl dies!"

They remained out in the waiting room, vying with each other to outdamn him. He might have ignored it but Judith was distressed. Then his phone rang and Dr. Whittaker, in the neighboring office, complained about the ruckus. Matt stood up abruptly, feeling his heart like a hammering fist in his chest. Judith sensed his violence. In her condition this conflict was a torture rack. He gave her a reassuring smile and slacked off as he moved to the door. He spoke to her parents in a conciliatory voice:

"Will you please calm youselves?"

Dirken glared malevolently. "I'll calmly report this incident and your threats of physical violence. Your occupancy of this office space amounts to an endorsement by the hospital. Men on the Board of Governors and the Chief Administrator are lifelong friends of mine. We'll not only bar you from the operating room, but terminate your office lease."

"Do your damnedest," Matt called as Dirken went out. "Meanwhile, in a more reasonable frame of mind, Mr. and Mrs. Chalmers, I want to point out something you're overlooking. She's determined to go through with the operation. Between now and the time she comes to the hospital she *must not be subjected to stress.* For that reason she'll not want to continue living at home."

"You can't get by with *that.*"

"Wait . . . please. I don't want her to leave home and break with you. It would be too great a wrench, too harmful to her. So, for her sake, will you go in there—I'll get

109

the young man out—and let her know that you're done fighting her about it and now want to do all you can to help her?"

"He'll take her to his family—well, if that's the family she wants, fine. We're leaving. But we're not quitting. We'll fight you to the last minute." They started for the door.

Matt moved around them. "Wait! Mrs. Metcalfe, will you see if Miss Tanner's in her office? Now, Mr. Chalmers, you can't walk out without a word to Judith . . ." Matt's voice dropped. "What if you fought till the last minute and lost, and what if the worst *did* happen, and the last words between you—"

"Miss Tanner's on the phone, Doctor."

"Elise? Matt. Busy? Well, could you possibly spare five minutes? . . . Yes, it's important . . . I'd appreciate it . . . Thanks, fine." He hung up, looked at the Chalmers. "I'd like you to speak to Miss Tanner."

Mrs. Metcalfe came over soothingly. "Won't you just sit down, Mr. Chalmers, Mrs. Chalmers?"

Matt went out into the corridor and walked down to the hall Elise would be coming along. In a minute she appeared, her fresh, snow-washed-looking face fretful, her sexy black bangs bouncing, her long sleek legs pummeling her skirt.

"What can I do for you, Matt?"

"Judith Chalmers is here, determined to go through with the operation. Her parents are dead set against it and we've just had a fight, during which I threw Dirken out of my office. They hate my guts so much I can't make them see the necessity of peace between them and Judith. A rift might traumatize the girl. If you can effect a reconciliation, Elise, it would be wonderful. Why, they want to walk out without even saying good-bye, and with a possibility of not seeing her before the operation—one which they consider very dangerous."

"And from what I hear *is* dangerous."

"If you're going in to reinforce that damned idea, don't go!"

She patted his arm and looked smilingly into his eyes. "I wouldn't do a thing like that, Matt. My goodness, you're upset, aren't you? Now you ease off, hear? I'll handle them."

And she did, putting on a professional performance for its own sake and for him, too, he knew. She shamed and

110

praised the parents in almost the same breath and before long she had the mother dabbing at her eyes and the father wilted.

When the parents left twenty minutes later the atmosphere between them and Judith was changed. He returned to a calmer Judith and began to prescribe medications and diet and to set up appointments for her in the outpatient clinic during the next week. When she left with her fiancé shortly after five, everything was set except the date she would enter the hospital.

A few minutes later Elise stopped in on her way home.

"How'd it come out?"

"Just fine, Elise. You did a nice job. I really appreciate it."

"It was nothing. Anybody but you could have got them to do what they really wanted to do in their hearts."

"Tell me, Elise," he said, laughing easily, "where, geographically, in the systems of preconscious, foreconscious, subconscious and unconscious, is the heart located?"

"One tries to communicate with the unwashed in their own language." She smiled. "Anyway, they promised not to badger the kid any more. I'm glad. And glad to give you a hand. Must rush, so bye now. And Matt . . ."

"What, minx?"

"Good luck."

"Thanks, Elise. Take care of yourself."

He was going to meet Vicky at 6:30. He didn't know how in the world he was going to tell her he'd broken his word about Judith.

It turned out he didn't have to. She arrived in his office, opened the door, stood there and hurled a small box at his head. She turned, sailed out through the waiting room at a run. He followed. She was stepping into an elevator. She flashed him an across-the-shoulder scowl and was gone. He went heavily back into the office. He picked up the little box. He opened it on the engagement ring, shut it, opened it and shut it again. He went out and locked the outer door and came back and sat down. He lay his head wearily on his arms on the desk. *I wish*, he thought, *I wish I could cry.*

During the next few days he phoned and she hung up; he went to her apartment and she opened the door only to

111

the end of the chainlock; he wrote a long, special delivery letter and sent two telegrams which went unacknowledged. He lurked at odd times, trying to catch her coming or going from her apartment, from her parents' home, from the store where she occasionally worked.

He followed her to a dance at the club where she affected an unconcerned, chatty, smiling manner, declining to show anger or to dance with him. She mingled with her crowd, explained her unengaged status with laughing casualness. She danced often and spread her charm indifferently among all, while he watched sickly from the shadows until he got sick of himself in that miserable role. He went out to their unfinished home at odd times, hoping to catch her in some sentimental moment. He didn't. But he found out she'd been there daily and had bribed the watchman not to tell him. He built that crumb of hope into a feast of significance. One afternoon he glimpsed her entering the hospital and rushed to his office.

He stopped in the doorway, suddenly bristling. Hank was standing there being charming and looking at her as at a slice of strawberry shortcake.

"Simmons, I stay out of your personal life," he snapped. "Keep the hell out of mine! You wanted to see me, Vicky?"

"Why, yes," she said in a little-girl voice. "Dr. Beaumont, I'm on the solicitation committee of the Ladies Auxiliary. We were wondering if you'd increase your pledge this year," she said, as they went into the inner office and Hank retreated. "Since you're a bachelor with no family expenses, we thought you should up it fifty per cent. You can pay in installments, or—"

"Vicky, cut it out!" He started to embrace her.

"Dr. Beaumont!" she said, widening her eyes and stepping back. "I'll send another girl."

On Friday he had horrible news about Merrijane Lacey. In addition to mitral stenosis she had a kidney tumor which might be cancer of a fast-spreading type. Her weak heart, her condition in general, ruled out two operations. A year would be needed before a second major operation could be risked. If he got the heart repaired her condition would improve and the time might be shortened to six months. The kidney tumor might not be cancer. But if it was the cancer he feared, Merrijane would be dead before six months.

112

He dictated a note to be attached to her case history, routed it to Drs. Coleman, Cape and Dielman for their opinions, wrote orders for four further lab tests. Uncertain about the value of one of them he went up to Pathology to discuss it personally. As he walked down the hall, he noticed a girl walking toward him. She wore partyish high-heels and the sheerest of nylons, but she was in an on-duty lab coat. The coat was open on a thin chiffon dress that clung like a spider web, nakedly revealing the intimate roundings of her pelvic area. Two interns had caught the scent and were close on the trail and she walked with plenty of hip action. She angled across the hall on a collision course with Matt and he caught the odor of whiskey and perfume.

"Hi," she said, and stopped.

Annoyed, he stopped sharply. Then he saw it was Vera Dell; her pretty, new face was lipstick-splashed, theatrically eye-shadowed and stamped with a vacant, silly expression.

"Vera!" he said in dismay.

The interns slowed down but kept looking back at her.

"Jussa minute . . ." she called and waved.

Matt gestured at them abruptly and they hurried off.

"Aw-w-w-w." Vera pouted. "Don't be an ole stuffy-wuffy."

"Now, Vera, you're going to get in trouble this way. I want you to go down to my office and out of sight. Tell the nurse I sent you. There're cots and—"

"Anything you say, doll, anytime you say."

"I'd better see that you get there," he said.

He walked her down and turned her over to Mrs. Metcalfe.

"Phone Pathology and report her sick. I'll tell them, too."

He almost forgot his business in Pathology concerned Merrijane. When he located the chief and started to tell him about Vera, he held up a hand and said:

"Don't tell me. Wednesday it was Arleigh Coleman. Yesterday, George Cape. She's 'fainted' three days in a row!"

"What? I didn't know this had happened before. This is serious!"

"Serious defect in the inventive power of you three guys. Come off of it, Matt. I know she's drunk—and turning into a nympho!"

"That's unjust!"

"I know, I know. Vera was a helluva good worker. I don't forget that."

"She will be again. When she smooths out. Give her a break."

"I have and I will. I love her, you love her, George and Arly and Al do, and we'll all try to gather round and protect her and carry her through this period, no matter how useless she is in this lab. But it's going outside this lab and endangering others.

"She's a free fall, Matt. I know of *five,* so far. This is unofficial, but your Shep Green's one of them. Your other boy's in the line. She can get a lot of interns in a lot of trouble. If they run afoul of the wrong doctor or official they can get bounced clear the hell out on their ass. So while we protect Vera—Well, you see. Get her in hand, for God's sake."

"I'll try. Now, I've got troubles; that mitral stenosis case . . ."

Matt remembered before leaving that Constanza had been hurt when he'd failed to say hello the other time. He stopped beside her, and when she turned that soft ballerina face and gave him a sweet slow smile, he felt an actual pang in his breast.

"And how's my friend, Constanza Vassily?" he asked.

"Sad-glad. I hope you're all right, Dr. Beaumont?" she said doubtfully, looking at him with too-perceptive, too-concerned eyes. He suddenly realized how much effort it required to turn from the warmth of her sympathy.

"I'm fine. Oh, you'll be interested to know it's all settled about our endocrine case. She's definitely scheduled to come into the hospital as soon as there's bed space."

"Oh, I'm so glad you told me. Oh, that's really good . . ."

Vera Dell was asleep when he got to his office. He made calls on Arly and George; Al was still out of town. They came to his office. When Vera woke they talked to her like Dutch uncles and she promised a little sulkily to at least be more careful.

Early Saturday evening Matt called in Shep and Hank and gave them an informal warning to leave Vera alone.

"As you both know, her case made enemies for me. One in particular—I needn't name him—would hit me from any

114

direction he could, so close connection with me puts you on a spot."

The phone rang and it was Vicky. He cupped the mouthpiece and repressed his impulse to grin half-wittedly till he got rid of Hank and Shep. Then, alone, he sat listening to Vicky offering to allow him back into paradise.

"Tonight?" he asked softly.

"This very minute, darling. You've had enough. I couldn't keep on when any further hardness on my part would be mere cruelty. I'm not up to that. Just as with you and that Hank Simmons, when he's done what he has to, you won't need to stay tough."

"When he's learned what he must, you mean?" he said, holding his breath.

"Yes," she agreed.

"So you think *I've* been taught *my* lesson and I'll come on my knees, Vicky? On your terms? Abandoning my patient?"

"Don't put it melodramatically. All that doesn't matter. What does matter is that I've missed you, I want you, lover . . ."

He hung up . . . very slowly, his face collapsing.

Sunday without her was grueling. He drove out of the city to nowhere in particular, planning to go far enough so that he couldn't get back till he made evening calls. But he was back before sunset, and wound up, as he'd been afraid he would, at their unfinished house. Emerging from the woods he saw her car. In the next instant he saw another car and tensed. He drove up the hill, his heart pounding.

He walked into the unfinished master bedroom. When he saw who it was with her he felt a double-twisting in his guts and an eye-blearing rage. He stopped and calmly removed his coat. Vicky, looking angrily ruffled, stood in the doorway to the deck.

Hank stood in the middle of the large room shaking his head and backing off. "Nothing was happening—"

"Not that you didn't try!" Vicky accused. "Matt, I didn't ask him here. I told him to leave!"

"Get 'em up," Matt said.

"Dr. Beaumont, I refuse to resort to physical violence, which solves nothing."

"I said defend yourself."

"I admit I went for her. To get at you where it hurt. But . . . *wait*—"

Matt walked toward him and Hank backed off till he came to a stop against one of the mirrors. Matt slapped his face.

Hank darted away. Matt followed implacably.

Hank crouched suddenly and, hissing air through his teeth, he brought up a blow from the floor, aimed murderously at Matt's head.

Matt took it on the arm. "Hate my guts, eh?"

"Yes!"

Hank smashed a left into Matt's belly. Matt backed off, jabbing at his face while Hank poured blows into his body, punched toward his head. Matt fended him off, watched and waited and abruptly rocked Hank's head with a smashing right to the jaw. He followed with a left uppercut, then another explosive right that tottered Hank, whose arms flew disconnectedly sideways. Matt drove rights and lefts into his chest and stomach and Hank sprawled.

When he got up, Matt drew back and brought his whole body pitching in behind his punch. The blow flattened Hank to the floor unconscious. Matt dragged him outside to the deck and was about to throw him off the deck when Hank came to, clawing, striking, kicking, coming up like a cat, peppering blows, light ones, hard ones, that made Matt grunt and retreat. Hank came on, hitting from a crouch, above and below the belt, anywhere and everywhere, fright-and-rage driving him.

Matt stumbled back, falling. Hank leaped on him, battering right, left, right, into his face, bloodying his nose. Matt rolled, dumping him off, then sprang to his feet and began a piledriver attack to body and head. He trapped Hank before one of the wall mirrors, bludgeoned his face so that the back of his head shattered the glass. Hank sagged, collapsing to the floor, mirror glass in his hair and on his clothes.

Matt walked away from him, wiping his bleeding nose. He went outside. When Hank roused and got to his feet Matt went back to him. Hank was feeling his face.

"Now, get out of here." Matt said. "I ever catch you with my woman again, Simmons, and I'll—well, just don't let me catch you!"

He followed him closely out to the car and watched till he pulled away.

When he returned to Vicky on the deck her green eyes glowed.

"You fought for me like a tiger. You love me crazy, Matt—face it!"

"I'm trying to face it—what that love does to me. And I know what you'd do to this house. Turn it into a club to show off in. My work would simply be the horse that pulls things. My work isn't in the service of anything but itself. It's never going to be subordinated to anybody. You included!"

She suddenly started to scream at the top of her voice. She kicked off her shoes and stamped her feet. "You'll do my way, Matt Beaumont, you'll do my way! Don't you dare work on that Chalmers bitch or I'll kill you. You hear me, you hear me!"

He stood emotionally frozen. She was waiting for him to handle her, to master her, to force her to yield. She knew she was on the wrong side. She wanted him, counted on him, to bring her safely into a decent position. But he couldn't. He wouldn't. He did not pity, nor love her in this moment, nor desire her.

"Make your decision, Vicky. I'll not come back. You'll have to come to *me*," he said, regretfully. "I can't bring myself to force you, to break your spirit, but you must learn, must know or . . ." he felt himself choking, ". . . or it would never work out. Think about it and decide, Vicky, It has to be my way, always."

He walked away from her. He turned his back on her. He thought his heart was going to break, and then he thought: *Cheer up, the worst is yet to come, the worst is yet to come.*

Chapter Ten

Word of the fight was all over the hospital by Tuesday, Matt couldn't walk down the corridors without encountering averted glances or open hostility. In the following days he caught glimpses of Hank parading his injuries in little groups, often with Dirken, his new friend, at his side.

Dirken and some cohorts were trying to build a big enough case against Matt to force him out of the hospital. He didn't care because word had come up from the admitting office that Judith would come into the hospital in two weeks; the use of the operating room was authorized for three days later.

Vera's conduct had changed a little, for the worse. He found himself called to the chief surgical resident's office. Shep was on the carpet. He'd been nabbed by Dirken coming out of Matt's office with Vera the night before.

"Dirken's coming in shortly, Matt," the chief resident said. "He wants to push it."

"Shep, I warned you, I told you, I—"

"I know." Shep looked forlornly out the window.

Matt gripped his shoulder. "Don't worry. How'd you get in the office? I'm really sore at you about that, Shep, sneaking in there . . . how long have you had a key?"

"I didn't!"

"Shep, I'm going to bat for you as hard as I can, but I must know."

"She had one. Vera. She said . . . well, *you* gave it to her." Shep looked embarrassed.

"I didn't. There's nothing between us. Now, listen, it's not you he's after. It's me. I'll give him me. Now, nobody actually *saw* you making love to her, did they? Just coming out the door at 11 P.M.? When'd you go in?"

"Ten twenty-five, and nobody saw us go in. She was across the street in the restaurant and I picked her up there, about ten."

"A date?"

"No. It just happened. I knew her, of course. Once before . . ."

"I remember you phoning me that she was in a disturbed condition. I had requested you to let me know whenever you observed this."

Shep's eyes widened, brightened. "Say, that's great, Dr. Beaumont."

Dirken came in, bustling importantly.

"Well, Dr. Beaumont, you see what your slut has done? The fine girl you and your accomplices turned into a 'beauty'? She's got this young fellow in serious trouble."

"Now, listen, Dirken, you've got nothing. Dr. Green was in my office with that patient on specific orders from me. His conduct there was beyond reproach."

"Oh my, Dr. Beaumont, you're not asking me to believe that! Even if this was by your order it's irregular enough to demand a formal charge be made. A male doctor alone at that hour with a female—"

"Alone? Why, my office nurse was there. I sent her at once. Do you want to check with her?"

"I won't ask the lady to perjure herself." He looked at Matt for a moment, then said: "Very well, I'll withdraw the charges."

"And maybe I'll withdraw a suit I'm preparing, Dr. Dirken—for slander and defamation of character, if I don't get any more reports of your poisonous remarks. Think about that, Doctor!"

He couldn't sleep Saturday night. He'd half dozed off at 2:30 when the phone bell made him jump half out of his skin.

"Hello!"

"Darling," Elise Tanner purred, "did you shave? My skin's all shuddery from thinking about your bristly chin."

"Get your esteemed chief to scrape you!"

"Don't growl at me."

Surprisingly, she began to bawl.

"What's wrong, Elise?"

"I'm a little drunk."

"Oh . . . well, sleep it off."

"And lonesome. And I hurt."

"Not physically?"

"No. Matt, my esteemed chief did come here once. I was

119

so pretty and wanted to please him. And he looked at me and he got on me in the bed like an animal. And all through it he looked down and poured dirt out of his mouth on me; filthy words, the nastiest, ugliest toilet words, as if that's what I am. But I'm not a bad girl, Matt, am I? Maybe a little bitchy, but not a dirty, filthy creature, am I?"

"Why, you sure as hell aren't. You're a first-rate girl, Elise. He's the filthy bastard. Don't you cry."

"Well, all right, if you like me."

"I like you."

"Matt, c'mon over."

"It wouldn't work. I can't help it, I'm just that way about somebody else."

"And it's bust, and you're suffering, and I think it's just terrible for you not to have a woman. It's crazy, Matt."

"I know."

"C'mon over. We'll have a drink and make love and feel good and—wouldn't you like to? Really?"

"Yes. I would."

"Will you come?"

"I will. I'm on my way."

Elise opened the door and immediately presented him with a double-whiskey on the rocks and a breath-taking eyeful of herself. Her nearly naked, long-lined body glowed with the exciting beauty of white fire under the transparent veil of a loose, floor-length white nylon robe, as fine as blown snow. Open networks of blue and silver net cradled her splendid, lifting, burgundy-nippled breasts and the cushiony softnesses of her lower belly, hips and buttocks. From the tips of her long pale toes, glinting with red polish, to her head, she was pure aphrodisiac.

She stood grinning up at him while he reached back to shut the door and lifted his whiskey at the same time. He drank it off and he hadn't set the glass down before she was in his arms. She put her mouth to his and her heat mixed with the whiskey fire in his throat and stomach and limbs. She kissed hot and put her whole body into the action, opening and closing her lips, inviting his deep kiss with flickerings of her tongue, and all the while her hips were rolling, her belly and her breasts gliding against him.

Breathless, she broke away and turned a half circle and walked into the center of the room and dropped her head back till her throat arched. She sucked breath loudly and, thrusting her arms stiffly straight down at her sides, she clenched her fists.

"Ooooh!" she said exultantly. "I'm a hot wild mare tonight! You stallion!"

He laughed. "You're gorgeous, Elise, just gorgeous."

"I'll drink to that! We'll drink to that! And for saying it, you darling, I'll give you eleven kisses!"

She touched her mouth with the fingertips of both hands then fluttered them over his face while giving him a light kiss on the lips. Then she turned and strutted over to the whiskey decanter.

When her moving back was toward him she swung her pert derriere enticingly and kept looking over one shoulder, flicking him with tantalizing little grins, checking for signs of excitement. Uncountable stimulating impressions of feminine curves and hollows, lines and angles, motions and gestures swarmed his senses and fused together into a powerful enchantment, and his hands craved the unforgotten feel of her. He wanted to rip through that floating veil of white nylon to her naked flesh.

Elise reached the table and sloshed whiskey into his glass and her own, standing with her legs spread, her upper body tilted slightly forward. Matt moved up behind her, hooked one arm around her waist and, pressing his spread hand into the softness of her lower abdomen, drew her to him. His other hand loosened the throat tie of her robe while she pressed back against him, rolling her bottom.

He pulled the robe down and kissed the slope of her shoulders and upper back and scraped her bare skin lightly with his beard. She shivered with pleasure and he felt a wave of tension run vibrantly through her whole body.

Keenly excited, Matt spun her roughly and gave her a long, hard kiss while he ran his hands, caressingly, possessively, over her soft warm body. She doubled her arms up her back and in a moment she flung the little bra away.

He took her breasts in his hands and squeezed and stroked their soft conical surfaces. She fastened her mouth hotly to his again. He stroked down the sweet, taut channel of her spine, then inserted his hands into the open net panties and palmed the cheeks of her buttocks and felt them clench at his touch.

She gasped and turned her face, panting. He spanned

121

her waist and lifted her onto the table, nearly spilling one of the poured drinks. She grinned shakily at him.

"Whiskey?" she asked.

"Who needs it!"

She dipped two fingers in a glass beside her and wet the taut, dark-purple nipple of one breast with whiskey.

"You sure?" she asked.

He laughed and put his lips to the nipple, flicked it quickly with his tongue, then nipped with his teeth. She sucked her breath in sharply.

"Harder! Bite!"

He stood up shaking his head. She took up her whiskey, sipped, rolling her black eyes up to watch him. He walked away, too stimulated.

She was sitting erect, her stomach sucked in till her lower ribs stood out, like dropping wings, and he noticed the groove running down her stomach past her long navel to the bright pink satin patch in the crotch of the net panties. She gazed at him and stroked her outspread hands up her body to her breasts. She lifted them high and lovely.

"Come here," she said, kicking at him and opening her knees. "Come and bite."

"You know I won't hurt your breasts."

"Oh, that mother-complexy thing of yours about breasts!" She hopped down from the table, fretfully.

He grabbed her, picked her up in his arms and carried her to the bedroom. She reached out and flipped a switch and the light blazed on a red satin bedspread so bright he had to blink. He flung her on her back on the bed and he ground his sharp-bearded chin against her ribs till she whimpered. He scraped a pink diagonal line down to her navel, up again to her ribs.

"Scrape me. Scrape me raw!"

She began to kiss his face passionately, her body writhing. When he hurt her again she cried out sharply, kicked and bounced frenziedly on the bed. She dug her fingernails in his shoulders; she clutched his hair. She moaned and gasped.

"Enough . . . enough," she begged.

When he stripped off her panties, a spasm ran through the flesh of her belly, and her thighs trembled. He stood up and undressed slowly, looking at her smooth, milk-white body squirming with desire on the bright red satin.

122

She lay with her eyes shut, breathing through open lips and moistening them every few seconds. Alternately she drew her knees up, tight together, then extended her legs full length. Her hands glided at her side over the red satin, her fingers sometimes clawing, trying futilely to get a grip on the slick surface.

She opened her eyes and saw him naked and fiercely passionate, and she reached out to touch him then rolled on her back, her belly sinking into the cradle of her pelvis as she tautened her muscles.

She rolled onto her stomach, onto her back again, and she locked her ankles and thighs together, trying to hold on. He delayed deliberately, heightening her craving till she was ready to scream.

She opened herself to him and when he entered her she began to lurch and kick with a jolting violence. She scratched him and tried to bite, and when he cuffed her she tried to kiss his hand. It was an intensity that left her drained. At the end she sprawled, her legs widespread. She stared gauntly at nothing and he stared at the bizarre wallpaper pattern of Rorschach ink blots.

She made him a good breakfast and sat across from him, a trifle puffy-eyed and hungover, having only coffee. When he lit a cigarette and said it was a good breakfast and she was good to look at, she dismissed it and asked seriously:

"Matt, I didn't get the right poop, did I, that you once knuckled under to Lassiter about that operation?"

"Well . . ." He shrugged. "Vicky was very upset . . . yes, I did."

"I can't believe it. No, I just can't, not about you." She looked out the window gloomily. "I guess you and I aren't, and never were, going anywhere. You'd never have knuckled under to me, even temporarily, on such a matter." She turned and looked worriedly at him. "And you *still* want her back?"

He dropped his gaze. "Elise, I don't want to hurt you. The missing element in my feeling toward you, even before I found out you didn't respect me——"

"I do, though." She reached over and squeezed his hand. "And I'm betting on you, but go on."

He returned the pressure of her hand, smiled gently at her.

"Thanks, minx. Well, that missing element that made it just short of love was that you're not in need of me, or anyone—"

"Oh, but I need just the same as any woman. I'm not that self-sufficient."

He frowned unhappily. "Well, that was my sense of you . . . I . . . Vicky, though, she's someone that loves me all out, and she needs all my love and protection. Oh, this makes my skin crawl—let me take you to dinner. I'd like to."

"Thanks. Sometime, maybe, but not today. You're hoping to reconcile with her, aren't you?"

"But only on my terms."

"But after the operation, with the issue past, you'll take her back? Yes?"

"You don't think much of me for it, do you? But you see she's emotionally insecure. That's all that's made her act this way. She's not really certain I love her."

"Oh, God, you've picked up some of our clichés—emotionally insecure, hell. She's *over*secure. Always had what she wants, always intends to get it. Which, of course, isn't my business. But I like you, Matt, and I'm afraid she'll wear you out. She'll impose her will, or try to, every chance she gets . . . to fight you on a thing like this is bad. It should warn you, Matt. Just what unconscious significance this girl has for you, which is stronger than your reason, I don't know, but it's something—O.K., O.K., I'll lay off. Let's have another cup of coffee."

When she got up and started away, Matt reached out and caught her arm and drew her back. She came unprotesting and sat across his knees. She gazed at him unhappily. "I always make you mad."

"Not this time. You hit a fact. Vicky does represent something—a bright-crackling, surging, beautiful life-force . . . the same thing you represented at first."

"At first!" she cried. "And then? You rejected everything I had to give you, except sex."

"It's all you wanted from me."

"I know less of your formative years than a stranger; you made me afraid of you," she said bitterly. "You know what you said to me one night? 'You're not going to perform emotional surgery on me without anesthetic'."

"I said that?"

"Yes. As if I'm cruel just because I say men choose an

ideal based on their first love." She hopped up and rushed into the bedroom. She came out with a box of tissues, dabbing her eyes. She zipped out a second and third tissue, blew her nose. "Now if I'd say your own mother was probably gay and bright and that in your search for the ideal you looked for that quality, you'd blast me. You'd talk like a moron who's not quite sure but suspects he's been accused of nastiness, or that dogs or Old Glory or motherhood has been insulted."

She kept walking around, agitated, zipping out occasional fresh tissues.

"Elise, wait. Listen—I couldn't have stood probing. If you'd cut down to that agony that I've spent my life fighting against I'd—oh, you don't know, you don't know."

"How *could* I know when you withheld everything a woman who is loved has a right to know? You wouldn't even try to let me understand you for fear I'd know too much."

"Because you wanted to fit my special problems into an all-purpose formula."

"I didn't."

"Listen! She wasn't gay, my mother. She wasn't bright and sparkling. She was abused, subjected to terror and violence. She was tears, Elise, sadness, distress. I loved her, oh, I loved her, but—"

He broke off. He went in the kitchen, found the whiskey and poured himself a stiff drink. She came and watched a little anxiously as he tossed it down.

She gripped his hand. "Go on," she urged, her black eyes piercingly alert on his face. "Go on!"

"When I was very small," he said tonelessly, "I wished a terrible thing. I wished I didn't love her, that I wouldn't be bound to her misery. I wished she wasn't my mother. I wished my aunt, her sister, would be my mother because—" He drew a long breath. "*She* had no tears, nothing but brightness and laughter and that surging, beautiful life-force. Do you see? I betrayed. In my heart I betrayed everything. I wasn't loyal to her pain, to the love I had for her and she for me. We both had the same enemy—"

"Your father?"

"See, your eyes gleam. You found I fit the formula—boy loves mother, is rival of father for her love. My hate for him sprang from fear he'd punish me for my guilty desires, eh? Had nothing to do with what *he* was, a terror who beat her and kept us afraid for our very lives, eh?"

"I didn't say that, Matt! You were too frightened and weak to protect her and a part of you turned to your aunt. You felt you were a betrayer, a deserter under fire."

"Something like that. She and her sister were killed in the same minute. I was nine. The chance to stand bravely in her behalf was gone. I sometimes think my whole ambition, my whole career has been an attempt to make it up to her, to bring her back, to be loyal to pain, not to fear it, not to turn and run, but to love it, give myself to it. Elise, you just told me Vicky has a hidden significance stronger than my reason. And so, I think, has Judith Chalmers. Against the reasoning and advice of my professional colleagues, I want to be brave for her, give her the sparkling aliveness that my mother was capable of— Now that you've opened this up, I'm not sure about the operation—"

"Oh, my God, if I've ripped you open on this thing, destroyed your adjustments and confidence, I think I'll die."

She began to sway, clutching her stomach, her eyes stark.

"No! You've *helped* me! Ive *got* to know what I'm doing. Not to know if it's medically valid or just some emotional necessity in me. But I can't see you again. Not till I've done that operation or not done that operation. Somehow that's the end of the world. I can't look past that day."

Chapter Eleven

Day after day and night after night Vicky didn't call, didn't come to him on his terms as he had been sure she would when she had had time to see the meaning of her position. She was, he thought, irresponsible, selfish, arrogant, shallow and small, and unworthy of a man's deep love. How damned lucky he was to know about her before he had irrevocably bound his whole future to such a creature!

He hoped she had fixed on another man—poor bastard, whoever he might be. He fumed and raged, then suddenly he would recall some mannerism, or expression or tone of voice or gesture and her whole exquisite being would blaze alive out of the empty dark and he would want to bellow like a wounded animal. He began to lose weight and appetite and sleep, for he would lie tensed, listening for a miracle, the sound of the phone bell.

If he could only hear her voice, just a "Hello, Matt, I'm all right. Good-bye." If only he could see her smile, touch her, hold her hand, kiss her. He began to have nightmares and had to resort to sedatives.

He had work, patients, problems or, he thought, he would have cracked. Wednesday he went for lunch in the big cafeteria. While one or two men at the long "surgeons' table" hailed him, many others did not. Matt found a corner table and sat facing a wall, eating sparely. After a while George Cape came over and sat down.

"Matt, do you have to antagonize *everybody* by ignoring them?"

"Who knows what his motives are and what they mean and if they're driving him to something or nothing?"

"The dark philosopher today, eh? He does have a lean and hungry look—he thinks too much. Ours not to reason why, but to do or die."

"How's Hank, since you took him over—doing or dying?"

"Simmons doesn't respond to me, either. Performs at about the level of a first-year intern."

Matt threw down his fork, pushed his food away.

"Congratulations, George. You told me I was ruining him. Now you're vindicated."

"Wasn't my intention to rub anything in. I've decided you're not to blame. I've decided to offer my services as first on the Judith Chalmers thing."

Matt's eyes widened. He started to grin. "Well, what do you know!"

"Took a closer look at those lab studies you did, then perused the endocrinologists' opinions. And most of all, I heard you're sticking her $25,000 for the job."

"Sentimentalist to the last! Mister, I'm honored to have you. She's coming in Monday. Operating next Thursday—week from tomorrow. I'll have to tell Judith about this. She'll be pleased, George."

"How is she?"

"Great. That little girl's got guts. I'm keeping in close touch—phone her twice a day, personal call every other day. The parents don't speak to me, but they're keeping their word not to plague Judith. You know I threw Tanner at them . . ." He chuckled. "She started punching below the belt and marched 'em in like lambs to make their peace. Well, I gotta run, George. Y'know I'm taking my calculated risk tomorrow with the kidney tumor—Merrijane Lacey, the mitral-stenosis case."

"Tough one. But if you get in and out fast with minimum stress to the system, the heart should hold."

"I'm sure of it. See you . . ."

He began the operation at 7:29, with Kwerlen, a resident, as first, Shep as second and Ruthie heading the nursing team. Bruce Fenton was using nerve-blocks and a light, general anesthetic. The lab had a special orderly standing by to take a specimen of the tumor.

Working in dead silence and tensely concentrating on speed, Matt reached the tumor before eight o'clock, excised a specimen, then set about the more tedious total removal.

The phone rang at 8:34. The word from the lab was negative. Matt received the information in a state of paralysis. Suddenly he broke, shouting through his mask:

"*Benign!* I risk a patient's life for a goddamned *benign* —"

128

"Matt," Bruce yelled. "Get hold of yourself—I'm losing the beat . . . she's stopped!"

"It's no damned use," Matt said hopelessly. "But give me the needle . . . the adrenalin . . ."

And of course, with Merrijane's heart, it was useless.

Twenty minutes later they wheeled her out with her face covered. Matt walked slowly out to the visitor's room to confront her father and her aunt, those loving, robust people who'd have given their whole strength to keep her weak body alive.

Matt stood and looked at them with such a toneless face that her father blurted: "Merrijane's dead!" He began to swallow rapidly. "Is she?"

Matt nodded slowly, his face ghostly. "I'm sorry, Mr. Lacey, Miss Lacey. Terribly sorry. You know that."

The aunt covered her face and sobbed quietly.

"I was almost done. I hadn't taken too long. But it was too much, too much stress on her system. I was afraid of that . . ."

"Yes. You said that. It was a risk—but that cancer would have killed her."

Matt spread his hands. "It wasn't cancer."

They looked at him stunned, unblinking, the aunt's eyes red, the father's dry. His mouth became bitter. Finally he said:

"You couldn't help it. We don't blame you, Dr. Beaumont."

"No," Merrijane's aunt said. "To show you—will you come to the services for her?"

"To the services? Oh . . . Yes . . ." he said confusedly. "Yes, thank you . . . thank you."

He turned over his remaining two operations to other surgeons. At noon the admitting office called to say his patient, Judith Chalmers, had been notified she could enter the hospital at once and the operation might be moved up to Monday. He phoned Judith and she was delighted that a room was available to her ahead of time. He hung up, shaking his head tiredly.

Judith was there by three, and he had to see her, but entering that room Merrijane had slept in the night before depressed him and he got away as quickly as possible.

He was in his apartment Friday night at 9:20 when the phone rang.

"Dr. Beaumont?" The girl's voice was breathless, unfamiliar.

"Yes."

"This is Vera—Vera Dell. You know, don't you, that I was fired—or as they called it, given a leave of absence? Permanent, I just know."

"No, I didn't know. But, don't be upset, Vera. We'll fix it—"

"I've used it all up fast, everybody's tolerance. There's no hope . . ."

"Slow down, be calm—"

"I can't. I'm desperate. Would you come? Please. I need you. It's only ten minutes from your place—would you?"

"What's your address?" He took down street and apartment number. "Just hold tight. I'm coming right away—"

"Oh, you're so good to me . . ." She began to cry.

He reached the small, brick apartment building in fifteen minutes. Surprisingly she was on the sidewalk in a short coat, dress, and pert jeweled beret. She ran to the car, opened the door hurriedly and got in.

"Drive away. Fast. Something terrible . . ."

"What is it?"

She scanned the cars parked on the other side of the street frantically.

"I don't see anybody, but drive away—go, hurry. They were to come a little after ten."

He drove down the block. "Who?"

"Listen. Detectives with cameras were coming to my place—to trap you, Dr. Beaumont. I was to get you there, try to get you to bed, or at least I'd get my clothes off. I'd leave the door unlatched; they'd come in—they offered me $1,000."

He turned onto an avenue. "Who did? What for?"

"I don't know who he was, but it's to stop that operation you're doing Monday."

"When you called, then, you were planning to trap me?"

She looked out her window. "I'm no good," she said flatly. "What I planned to do to you, and the way I've disgraced all of you who believe in me proves it."

Matt took a long breath. "You did back down on this."

130

"When I started to cry over the phone, that's when I knew I couldn't. I'm so ashamed, Dr. Beaumont." She started to cry again.

He wanted a place to stop and turned into a drive-in. A waitress came.

"Two hamburgers and coffee."

"Everything on them? Cream in the coffee?"

"Yes, fine."

"Instead of telling you not to come, I wanted to warn you to be careful. And also I wanted you to know what I am and not have any more hopes about me."

"We can't give up hopes about you. You know you're our project. We *can't* let you down, and we have no desire to. We never dreamed when we started all this that anything but good could result, that you'd be anything less than happy—well, we all do things we regret. You couldn't stab any of us in the back, Vera, or even consider it—not the real you, the one we tampered with. Grown men playing with dolls, that's what we were. It's our fault."

Their orders came. She wanted nothing, but took the coffee. He unwrapped one of the sandwiches, then left it untouched.

"Maybe, inadvertently, you saved a life tonight. The one I was to operate on Monday. My reason for wanting to change *that* girl is—I don't know, tampering with a life, playing God—"

"Oh, you *mustn't* stop just because I went bad—oh, that's unfair, unjust. You mustn't talk this way. I just hate myself if I've helped defeat you. Why, it's worse than if I'd gone through with that horrible plan. You look so worn out, Dr. Beaumont, it's a shame. Oh, why did I tell you!"

"We're neither of us beaten. But you've got to quit thinking of your new face as a mask."

"A mask?"

"Yes. In primitive tribes they put on masks for certain occasions. They're free then to violate all their taboos because the masks made them somebody else. But you're not somebody else, Vera; what you do counts. I don't believe you can make your new adjustment in the old setting, in contact with all the people who knew you before. They'll never see the new face unconnected with what it was. I think you sense that everyone can see through your 'mask.'

In another environment, another city, another job—we'll get one for you—no one will think of your face as anything special. It's just that of a pretty girl, nice to look at, and they'll accept it literally at face value. You'll be more relaxed, free from compulsions to prove anything to them, or yourself in relation to them. What do you think?"

"What I wanted that money for was just that. To get away, to run away, to quit—so I couldn't ask my doctors, my best friends for help in not facing my problems here."

"The longer you stay here, the more you complicate; the deeper you get, the more agitated and damn foolish you'll act. We'll go to your place. I'll call Dr. Horner, and Coleman and Cape, and between us all, we'll get you set."

He flashed his headlights, started the engine. When the waitress picked up the tray, he started back to Vera's apartment.

"But those detectives are coming!"

"They'll find me clothed and in the hall."

Apparently they knew he was alerted. They didn't show up.

By Sunday morning Vera had chosen her city—Chicago. Arley had phoned a lab director there and got the job for her. Al had found her an apartment there with a woman friend of his. George and Matt attended to her transportation. The four of them had lunch with her at the airport, where they gave her advice, instructions, money, assurances and orders to phone them at once if she hit any snags.

They took her to the gate and when she waved, just before vanishing into the plane, they waved back solemnly. They stayed till the flight was safely aloft, not looking at each other. Al took out a dime, flipped it in the air, and let it fall to the floor.

"Heads or tails?" he wondered. But the coin rolled down the ramp. Nobody went to look.

The service for Merrijane was at three o'clock in a mortuary chapel. He arrived as late as possible. He almost never went to funerals, and when he had to go he only seemed to look into the casket. Approaching Merrijane's, he angled his head down and shut his eyes. His stomach began to knot, his breath was tight in his chest. He knew they flanked him, the father and the aunt. They were watching him. He had to look; he had to look at her dead face. His head began to ache violently. Gripped by a morbid compulsion and sense of guilt, he joined the cortege to the cemetery and remained till the casket was lowered into the ground.

In his apartment he watched the sunset, a great smearing of orange color from which the light bled slowly until it was purple, then gray, then black. He had to wrench himself out of stupor to get to the hospital.

He reached the hospital and went up to the eighth floor. By-passing the nurses' station and speaking to no one, he made his way along the busy corridors and entered Judith Chalmers' room. Her father, mother and fiancé were there. He was briefly civil to them for Judith's sake, then he absorbed himself with her chart for several minutes.

Her parents and her fiancé left the room. Judith, mildly sedated, was semi-reclined in the bed, her pillowed head surrounded by the lovely mist-light of her blond hair. She smiled at him and her blue-gray eyes shone. He drew up a chair and they spoke in soft banalities, for there was nothing more to say. Just before he left an expression like a dark whisper brushed her thin, long face and she reached out and took his hand.

"It's all right, Dr. Beaumont?"

He touched her cheek, very briefly, his eyes infinitely tender.

"It's all right, Judith. My word of honor."

It was nearly ten when he left the hospital. It was a warm night. He was cold. He needed warmth, softness, sweetness. He didn't know if she was home, or if she'd let him in. But he *had* to see her. Even if it meant waiting an hour, two hours. His sense of urgency was extreme. His heart was actually racing when he stopped at her door. His fingertips were cold. If she wasn't home or if she didn't let him in he didn't know what he would do. Nothing had ever seemed so important in his whole life. If she was home but with another man, he'd . . . well . . .

He knocked.

She opened the door to the end of the chain-lock and peered out.

"Oh, it's you, Dr. Beaumont. I wasn't expecting any-one."

"I'm sorry to barge in on you, Constanza . . . could I talk to you?"

"If you'll give me a minute," she said, opening the door, "to get a little more presentable. Come in."

"Thanks."

He'd never seen her informally. Her hair was tied in a pony tail and she wore blue shorts, a yellow sweater and white ankle socks without shoes. The bathroom door was partially open, revealing lines of intimate laundry: stockings, panties of various colors and bras. She must've washed her last bra; it was unavoidably obvious that she wore none; her breasts under the light sweater were unconfined and fuller than he'd suspected—in fact, they were models of opulence.

The apartment was small, a little overcrowded. She led him to an overstuffed chair angled toward a coffee table and sofa-bed. She excused herself and went across to a closet and chest of drawers.

She moved with casual natural grace, her heels slightly lifted, her slim, supple feet springy, her knees loose. By the time the motion reached her hips it was absorbed, for there was no jolting, just an easy rolling of her hips and pelvis. Taller than Vicky, broader than Elise, she could not match their figures in certain particularities, but he did know that a woman did not come in pieces. She was a whole. And in Constanza the whole was suffused with an essence that was greater than definable beauty.

She slipped into the bathroom with the clothing she had gathered. When she returned a few minutes later, she was wearing a loose white blouse, a voluminous, flowered skirt and a wide belt defining her trim waist.

"How charming you look, Constanza," he said. He stood up, smiling uncertainly.

"Thank you. Would you like coffee?—oh, I have some wine!"

"Nothing, really . . . if you want something, of course, don't let me stop you."

"No." She seated herself at one end of the sofa-bed.

Matt hesitated between the armchair and sofa-bed. He sat in the middle of the sofa-bed.

134

"I know this is barging in on you, Constanza."

She shook her head slowly. "You know I want you," she said.

"I left the hospital in a state of real need for you. I just had to come and be with you—you heard about my losing a patient?"

"I was sorry, Matt. I kept hoping you'd call me, or drop in at the lab . . ."

"I wanted to. I didn't because I thought, 'What kind of a friend am I, always going with trouble to unload?' But I went to that patient's funeral today . . . and there were other things. Our endocrine operation is tomorrow morning, and it's like I had death at my back and maybe just ahead, and I—I had to see you."

"Your friend, Constanza Vassily?"

Her ballerina face was like a night flower, touched with moonlight. He felt again the silent pull of her, the passive force, the instinctual power of this woman, her depth and softness and warmth. He was drawn to the glow and fullness of those dark eyes, the sweetness of her upper cheeks, the slight trace of sadness about her pretty lips, with that faintest droop at the corners.

She was a friend, a precious friend, and a beautiful woman. He looked at her, yearning to touch her, to feel the sweet, warm softness of her mouth, to absorb her sadness, to lift her and himself.

She sat on one hip in a corner of the sofa, her legs drawn up under the voluminous flowered skirt and gazed at him. As he moved to her there was a flicker of motion around her eyes, the faintest widening, then a relaxation. He expected her to flow toward him, her mouth seeking his as his sought hers. But her head moved almost motionlessly back away from him, a yielding and a retreat that came to a stop against the back of the sofa.

She received his kiss and lay under him. He withdrew and she watched him, her lips apart, surrendered, waiting He saw and felt her contentment and he moved to her again and withdrew again, just to look at her. She smiled a little, very tenderly, and stroked his face with a breath-soft touch of her fingers. There was power in that touch, as if she had reached to his depths, had felt his need, had touched it with exquisite delicacy, and had stated in that touch all that was precious to him.

"Not my friend, Constanza Vassily, but the woman I love."

"I am your beloved," she murmured, "and I am well loved. And I've known it, my darling, for so long—almost as long as I've loved you."

"You still do? Oh, God, what a relief!"

Chapter Twelve

Matt was in the hospital by six. He felt fresh, strong, alert. He had a final huddle with George, then twenty-five minutes alone, visualizing for the final time the operations on Judith which were to come. He had anticipated everything, he was confident every conceivable problem was solved in advance.

The preparations in Operation Room A were extensive. Even with a double team of nurses and two extra orderlies and the assistance of the resident Kwerlen, who was going to stand as second, it was a quarter to eight before the tables were ready with sterilized instruments, sutures, needles, supplies, solutions, medications and drugs for the major laparotomy and the thyroid work.

He moved within and above the orderly chaos, watching hawkishly, speaking in terse monosyllables. When Judith was brought in at 7:20 he assisted Bruce with a spinal block. By 7:50 she was on the table, draped, unconscious, and Matt, silently withdrawn, was in the scrub room beside George, who was equally silent. Nurses standing by helped them into their gowns, caps, masks and gloves.

In addition to extra tables and working personnel and standard equipment in the big room, an overhead mirror on a roller base had been brought in to accommodate the observers who had requested permission to watch. They stood, seven of them, including two senior surgeons, a resident, Shep—and Hank Simmons. They stood in an irregular formation, white-masked and green-gowned but ungloved, unscrubbed.

Their eyes alternated between him, George, Judith's laparotomy-sheeted body and the mirror, which was angled to show the reddish circle of anticepticised bare skin exposed by the hole in the sheet. Matt walked toward the operating table with a sense of traversing a jungle into a clearing, where a core of brilliant, glareless light, focusing upon a supine, unconscious girl, gave the occasion a heightened reality and mystery.

He sensed himself, red-gloved and faceless but for his intense, deep-set dark eyes, as a figure presiding over some exalted ritual—not of sacrifice but resurrection. Tubes from infusion and transfusion bottles, suspended on high stands, penetrated her arm which lay inert on a support running out at right angles from the operating table. What looked like an instrument of suffocation, the rubber mask on her mouth and nostrils, was actually breath. The small, glass-encased breathing assistor pumped in a steady, easy rhythm with a polite little hum and soft gasping.

He looked at her closed, pale-lashed, translucent eyelids and visualized the blue-luster brilliance waiting to shine with full life in her blue-gray eyes. He smiled very faintly, then moved back to the center of the table.

Matt sent a scanning glance out at the waiting nurses, orderlies and the observers on the perimeter of the table, then narrowed his focus in to Ruthie, Kate Summers, Kwerlen, George. He seemed to teeter for just an instant at the edge, his tension so much sharper than usual that it reached out to the others, holding them, their watching eyes transfixed.

"Ready, George?"

"Yes."

He stepped up. The equipment was rolled in. Ruthie swung the Mayo stand tray out over Judith and at Matt's nod she slapped a knife handle into his glove.

Speed, but control, he warned himself. He and George moved like four hands on a single nervous system, and Kwerlen came in ready when needed and stayed the hell out of the way when that was needed. Ruthie and Kate were alert, anticipating every need.

They moved quickly; the bleeding was kept to a minimum, clamps on and off in record time, retractors placed. George's needlework was a pleasure, but when he began to talk in a stacatto voice, describing what they were doing, Matt wanted to tell him to shut up; he restrained himself. Her flesh was young, her organs vital, the slick, resilient rich-blooded arteries were throbbing steadily.

The tone and appearance of the nerve tissue and muscle fiber were not only promising but almost a guarantee that her basic good health would pull her through. Once she was in balance and did not function in short spurts of uncontrolled vitality followed by long exhaustions; when she

138

was past these continual stresses, this eternal pattern of overcompensations, she would live as a woman had the right to live.

The fulcrum of the problem was her adrenal glands. The blood supply and innervation was overly profuse, giving rise to excessive adrenocortical secretions and disturbance of the total system. One of the consequences was gonadal involvement, and though the ovaries themselves were normal they alternately over- and under-functioned.

Theoretically the lessening of the arterial supply to renals and adrenals, and the removal of a portion of nerve tissue was simple. The actual work was exquisitely tedious and time-consuming. Matt was in constant tension, fighting to dam the flooding pressure of time. At 10:30 he and George had to walk away for a smoke in the scrub room; they had been operating for over two hours. Then they quickly rescrubbed and returned to the table.

The trick in this whole business was the necessity to do a second operation immediately, to open her throat and excise portions of thyroid and, more dangerously, two of her parathyroids. The calcium-balance problem was aggravated by the work on the adrenals; tetany complication and postoperative shock were the most serious dangers.

They weren't through with the first operation till 11:30, a full hour behind his planned schedule. She seemed fine, breathing easily, blood pressure normal, pulse strong.

"Paint her throat, Ruthie, we're going to cut it," he ordered.

He looked over incredulously to where the gallery of observers had been. Not a one of them was there.

"What the hell—when did they leave?"

"Hour ago," Kwerlen told him. "There was a furnace explosion out at the K. and D. Ironworks. They sucked all the doctors they could get out of every hospital in town. A hundred injured, twenty fatalities so far."

"Well, there's nothing I can do. I can't leave."

It was two o'clock when they finally wheeled Judith out into the recovery room. Matt went into the scrub room, pulled off his mask and gloves, and sank exhaustedly on a stool there, elbows on his knees, his face in his hands. He was groggy, a little dizzy. After five minutes he got up and went into the recovery room and went on vigil with the nurse and resident.

He had food and coffee sent in. He didn't want to leave her for one minute, not for ten or twelve hours. He sent out word to her fiancé that all had gone well.

Judith started to come out of anesthetic around four. He gave her morphine and took a walk out to the visitors room. There was a hubbub of anxious people milling around, evidently families of the dozen or so furnace blast victims who'd come to NSG. Emerging from the crowd, Mr. and Mrs. Chalmers approached him anxiously.

"I suppose," Matt said coldly, "her fiancé told you it went well. At present she is resting easily." He turned and walked away from them.

The operating room supervisor caught him on his way back to Judith.

"Dr. Beaumont, will you tend to the authorization in writing? I've only got the verbal now—"

"What authorization are you talking about?"

"Why, Dr. Simmons'. This morning. There was no one here to handle an emergency gall bladder case who was brought in unconscious. Everyone had gone to the factory explosion—you *did* authorize . . .?"

"Send Simmons to the recovery room with the authorization slip. I want to talk to him."

Waiting for Hank he went over and checked Judith, then went to the door. Hank came fifteen minutes later, hurrying, his head down. He stopped before Matt, looked at him, fright in his eyes.

"What the hell did you pull? I didn't authorize you to operate on anybody." Hank said nothing. "Well?"

"No, that's so. I know you didn't. I lied."

"I didn't mean I want an explanation about you. I know you didn't have authorization; I know you lied. I meant, how's the patient?"

"She's good. Fine. Recovery normal."

"Why'd you use my name? Why not George Cape?"

"I didn't think."

"Did you bring the authorization slip?"

"I tore it up."

"Well, get the hell back and get another one."

"You're going to sign it? You really will?"

"Why, you're damned right. I've been trying to get you to use your God damn guts and stick your neck out. You don't think I'm going to turn around and punish you for it."

Hank began to grin, then to laugh. "Thank you, Dr. Beaumont. Would you accept my apologies for . . . well, for everything?"

Matt grinned at him. He put out his hand.

"Shake, kid. I'm beginning to have real hopes for you, Hank!"

At eight o'clock he telephoned Constanza.

"Listen, sweetheart—" he began.

"I'm listening, lover."

"I'm riding real high, but I'm scared to leave her. You understand I'd rather be with you than with anybody in the world, don't you, Constanza?"

"I do, and I love you and I'm proud of you and—oh, Matt, I just can't wait . . . but yes, I can . . ."

At midnight Judith was conscious and in her room. He stood by the window. He heard her stir. He went over. She was smiling. And smiling harder. Panic caught his guts. It stretched, that smile, toward ghastliness, toward a grisly horror, the characteristic grin of tetanus! But, in this case, tetany . . . soon the convulsions would begin . . .

Her smile relaxed, narrowed, softened. She sighed.

"Hello."

"Can you sleep?"

"Yes."

Around two he went down to his office and slept. He was up again in an hour. He went back to Judith. The special nurse nodded, and held up her fingers in a V.

At eight o'clock he went out into the visitors room for the fifth time. He woke her fiancé. He winked at him.

"You want to go look at your girl?"

"You think the danger period's really over?"

"I do!"

Matt was in Pathology when Constanza walked in.

"What do you think you're going to do today? Work?" she asked.

That sweet face, the moonlit, night-flower face, that adorable ballerina face began to smile slowly. She lifted one lovely, languid little hand, palm up. He smiled at her.

"What is the desire of my man?"

He took her outstretched hand, and walked her out, keeping a tight grip on his woman.